BARBARY SLAVEGIRL

by

ALLAN ALDISS

SILVER MOON BOOKS LTD

The BARBARY Series by Allan Aldiss

(To be published by Silver Moon)

Barbary Slavemaster
Barbary Slavegirl
Barbary Pasha
Barbary Sheik

Also from Silver Moon:-

Erica, Property of Rex
Circus of Slaves

For specimen chapters and publication details of forthcoming Silver Moon titles please leave name and address on our 24 hour phone line. (No charge other than phone call)

0891 - 310976

(Calls charged at 36p per min Off Peak: 48p per min at all other times)

or write to:

Silver Moon Readers Services, P.O. Box CR25, Leeds LS7 - 3TN

(New Authors welcomed)

Copyright of Allan Aldiss 1993
ISBN 1 897809 03 4

BARBARY SLAVEGIRL

CONTENTS

Chapter		Page
1	Shipwrecked	10
2	Captured	17
3	My first taste of slavery	24
4	Hassan Ali's estate	33
5	Preparation for inspection	38
6	The selection	45
7	Rejected	52
8	Processed	57
9	The feeding trough	63
10	Brothel training and the Bey	77
11	Advanced training	81
12	Pageboys	89
13	The Bey and the Bastinado	92
14	Sent to market	98
15	The night before the sale	104
16	Prepared for sale	108
17	Examined in the exhibition hall	114
18	The Auction ring	121
19	The silver cage	125
20	The raffle	133
21	The winners get their prize	141
22	The Friday beatings	147
23	The banquet	153
24	Serving the Bey	158
25	The galley	167
26	The slave pens	173
27	Branded	179
28	Life as a galley slave	186
29	Used for the Bey's pleasure	192
30	Sent to the Bey's harem	198
31	The master returns	202

AUTHOR'S NOTE

This story takes place at a time when European girls really were captured by the Barbary Corsairs and sold in the slave markets of North Africa.

Such women really were totally at the mercy of the rich men who owned them, and of the black eunuchs who supervised them. The Barbary States did have a reputation for treating Christian slaves unbelievably harshly, almost as animals, and there actually were slave breeding farms in the Ottoman Empire ... and although you won't find Marsa on the map, it could well have been there.

The principal naval powers were busy fighting each other - the long drawn out war between Britain and Revolutionary and then Napoleonic France started in 1793 and only ended with the battle of Waterloo twenty-two years later - and this gave the Corsairs great freedom of action. This period also saw the elimination of one of their main enemies, the Knights of Malta. Thus, at the time of this story, the Corsairs had an almost free rein to plunder and kidnap along the coasts and islands of Southern Europe.

By this time they had replaced their sea-going galleys with fast sailing craft such as Polacca-Chebecs, which carried a mixture of European style square sails and Arab style lanteen sails. The demand for large numbers of young male Christian galley slaves had therefore dwindled. Instead, many of the Corsos, as the raids were called, concentrated more on capturing young women and boys.

In 1798, for instance, only a few years before the setting of this novel, Barbary Corsairs from Tunis carried off almost a thousand women and children in one raid on the island of San Pietro, off Sardinia. Years later some were ransomed, but many had been sold off in the slave markets and were never seen again.

So although what follows is fiction, the background is realistic and those of a squeamish disposition are advised not to read the books in this series.

For a more serious study of the period I would recommend books such as Stephen Clissold's 'The Barbary Slaves' (Elek Books), Noel Barber's 'Lords of the Golden Horn' (Macmillan), 'Harem, the World Behind the Veil' by Lytle Croutier (Bloomsbury), and books about the Knights of Malta.

PROLOGUE

It was early in 1810 that I, renegade Irishman though I was, found myself being sent to Malta on a delicate mission by my superior, the Pasha of Marsa, a port on the North African coast.

I made quite a stir when, attended by Tulip, my page boy, I strode into the crowded ballroom in the former palace of the Grand Masters in Valletta, where the British Commissioner, Captain Sir Alexander Ball, had invited me to a ball he was giving.

I was in my somewhat exotic full dress uniform as a senior officer of the Janissaries, the elite troops of the Turkish Empire: blue embroidered tunic, yellow boots, baggy Turkish shalwar trousers and a strangely shaped tall felt hat surmounted with Birds of Paradise plumes.

It was there that, later in the evening, I was accosted by this fiery Irish girl, Barbara Kennedy.

"So, Sir," she demanded, almost as soon as she was alone with me, "you call yourself an Irish gentleman!"

"Indeed!" I replied.

"And what sort of an Irish gentleman is it who is no more than the disgraced scion of one of your wretched penniless Protestant ascendancy families!"

I started back. Evidently I was talking to a Catholic with strong Republican views. It was of course only ten years since the Wexford Rebellion, the Battle of Vinegar Hill, and the death of Wolfe Tone.

"And is it not true," she went on, "that you who call yourself an Irishman have a harem of Arab wives?"

I could feel my face beginning to cloud with anger at this pretty woman's ill-mannered approach. Her aggressive attitude made me a little more provocative than I would normally have been, and for a moment the discretion that my mission demanded was forgotten.

"Not wives, Miss Kennedy," I replied coldly. "Not wives! Concubines is the correct term for them. Concubines, if you please."

"Concubines!" she cried. "Concubines, is it! You mean slaves, no doubt! You mean you keep a harem of slave girls? You'll be telling me next that you beat the poor creatures when the fancy takes you."

"My black eunuchs certainly beat them if they do not please me," I said. I was controlling myself with difficulty, for it was intolerable for this rude and outspoken chit of a girl to broach such private matters in public.

"Oh!" she shouted out loudly, so that people turned to stare at us, "black eunuchs is it now! Holy Mother of God, what a monster you are! It's just as well it's only ignorant Arab girls that you have!"

"As a matter of fact, Miss Kennedy," I said, really angry with her now, "I, like, most other Moslems in my position in Marsa, where I come from, have several beautiful and well educated Christian girls in my harem. Some of them look very like the ladies here tonight and two of them are very like you!"

The Irish girl spluttered and went white with passion. She stamped a delicate foot in outrage, but seemed unable to speak. "Like me!" she got out at last, "LIKE ME!"

She was glaring at me so fiercely that I almost took a step backwards. Instead I looked straight into those fiery eyes. "Like you," I repeated. "More polite, of course. Prettier, perhaps!"

She gulped and paused to regroup, then changed her attack, as women will.

"I don't believe a word of it ... and what about this pretty page-boy?" She pointed at Tulip who was standing dutifully behind me. "Just where he does he fit into this story of barbaric lust?"

"His name is Tulip. The Turks would call him a 'garzon'. He accompanies me everywhere, especially when I am travelling or visiting the women in my harem."

"Oh! Oh! You brute! You brute!" Again she stamped a delicate foot. I dare say I would have found her attractive under other circumstances - once she had learned to keep a civil tongue in her head. "So you really are a Moslem, now!"

The way she spat out the word Moslem made it into an insult, but I   still held my temper in check.   My attachment to that religion was really only skin deep, little more than a convenience, but I was damned if I was going to say so to this rude little bitch of a girl.

"A Moslem?" I repeated. "Yes indeed, I am a follower of the true Prophet. I am proud of it, just I am also proud of owning my European concubines, slave girls captured by the corsairs and sold in the slave markets of Marsa. You can look as shocked as you like, but in the eyes of a True Believer they are mere infidel Christian dogs to be used for whatever purpose their Master may decide ... But, my dear Miss Kennedy, I should add that no matter how cheap European slave girls may be in Marsa, I doubt if any high ranking Turk there would wish to add a nasty little spitfire like you to his collection. So you would be quite safe, if you were ever captured. You'd probably just be used as a beast of burden, part of the live-stock of some farm."

"You swine! You miserable wretch of an arrogant Protestant land-owning swine!"

She was screaming at me, quite out of control.

Unfortunately I laughed, and it was then that she made a real enemy of me.

She actually had the temerity to to strike me on the cheek, twice, with her glove.

And I could not lift a hand to her, not in that company! No, I had to contain my fury as best I could, knowing that they were all sniggering at me - but also knowing that my mission would be prejudiced, perhaps irretrievably ruined, if I reacted in any way.

"I shall not forget this, Miss Kennedy," I murmured quietly. "I hope for your sake that our paths do not cross in the future."

Then I bowed and walked away, leaving her speechless.

She certainly needed to be taught a few sharp lessons in civility and respectfulness. Little did I think then that I was later to help provide them, nor that she would end up ... as she has done.

I commanded her to write down her story in her own words. I think you will enjoy it more than she did ...

PART ONE

I BECOME A SLAVE

Chapter 1

SHIPWRECKED

Just as I thought I would drown in the rough seas, I suddenly felt myself flung onto a sandy beach. With what seemed to be my last ounce of strength I struggled against the undertow - and won!

Slowly I crawled up the beach out of reach of the surf. It was pitch dark. The gale shrieked, blowing the sand along in its wake. I found myself in a little half sheltered dip with long grass around me. Exhausted, I collapsed onto the soft sand, still spitting out the sea water that I had swallowed.

Was I alone, I wondered, in surviving the shipwreck? The fishing craft, a luzzu, had been caught in a Gregale, the sudden fierce North Easterly Gale that could sweep down across the straits between Italy and North Africa. Forced to flee before the wind, the little craft had been blown down towards the Barbary Coast.

Suddenly in the heaving darkness she had hit a rock. In a few minutes she had broken up. The three Maltese fishermen had been swept overboard. Luckily I was a good swimmer, thanks to holidays spent on the wild West coast of Ireland when I was a young girl. I just had time to to get most of my heavy clothes off, before I too had been swept into the raging sea, leaving all my possessions to the elements.

Too exhausted to think, I curled up in the shelter of my little dip in the beach and fell asleep.

It was daylight when I awoke. The wind had dropped and the sun was shining. My only garment, a thin shift, was almost dry. I could hear the surf still pounding on the beach. I raised my head and saw an empty beach between two headlands. Some hundreds of yards out to sea was a spray covered line of rocks where the fishing boat must have foundered, but there was no sign left of her, apart from a few planks on the beach.

I stood up, shaky and weak from my ordeal, naked except for my shift. I called the names of the fishermen. There was no reply, and no sign of them. I was alone, quite alone. I walked along the beach, looking for any signs of my possessions.

There were none.

No one would know what had happened to me, not the authorities in Malta, not my employer in Sicily, and not my family or betrothed back in Ireland. I, and the crew of the fishing boat, would simply be assumed to have perished in the storm.

I was twenty four, a well educated but poor Catholic Irishwoman, who bitterly resented the British occupation of my country. I was regarded as a pretty young girl, and my cousin, Dermot, had asked me to marry him as soon he inherited his Great Uncle's farm. But meanwhile, to earn my living, I had taken the post, two years before, of Governess in the household of the British Ambassador to the Court of the King of Naples. In fact King Ferdinand had been forced by French troops to flee to Palermo in Sicily several years previously, and there he was protected by British troops and by the Royal Navy. Meanwhile the French had set up a puppet King of their own in Naples, first Joseph, Napoleon's older brother, and then Marshal Murat, his brother-in-law.

I had gone to Malta to buy English books for my young charges. A few days after that awful scene with the Irish Bey, I found a Maltese fishing boat that was leaving for nearby Sicily and persuaded them to take me as a passenger, so that I could get back to my employers.

And now here I was shipwrecked somewhere in Barbary!

Barefoot and walking with care, I started to make my way inland, following a path that led up to a small hill. I was hungry and thirsty. I came across a little stream, leading down towards the beach, and drank eagerly. But I was still hungry as I continued up the path.

At last I reached the top of the hill, and looked down the other side. Some fifty feet below me was a little gorge and, a track running through it, and I saw the marks of wheels.

Civilisation!

Indeed I soon heard the noise of wheels approaching. I was about to run down to the track when I remembered that I was half naked and in the Barbary Coast. Hesitantly, I lay down in the long grass, and hidden from the track, looked down into the gorge.

Into view came a typical Mediterranean two wheeled country cart, pulled by a donkey. It was laden with farm produce: vegetables and live chickens in wooden cages - all apparently being taken to market. Driving it was a Negro in a long brown robe and a coloured turban.

But it was the girl who caught my eye. She was running along behind the cart. A light chain ran from the back of the cart to an iron collar fastened round her neck. Her wrists were also loosely chained, and she was trying to hold a shawl over her shoulders.

Except for the shawl she was naked.

The Negro driver paid no attention to her as he occasionally plied his whip to the donkey. The girl made no protest as she ran along behind the cart. It was if she was used to being treated just as another animal being taken to market.

Her skin was white.

I shivered with fright.

Tortured by thoughts of slavery, I lay in my hiding place, warmed by the autumn sun.

Next a cavalcade of horsemen trotted past me. They were richly dressed, riding beautifully schooled and harnessed Arab horses. They were laughing and chatting in high pitched voices as they rode behind and in front of a bearded Moor with a huge blue turban, who seemed to be their chief. His attendants were youths, rather pretty youths, with beardless European complexions and wearing the same strange conical hats that I had seen the Bey's page-boy wear at the British Commissioner's Ball in Malta.

Riding behind them was a powerful looking Negro. In his hand he held a short whip.

I gasped as I saw that on either side of the bearded man's horse, ran a pretty white girl. They both wore simple white tunics and sandals. A delicate silver chain ran from each side of the man's saddle to a silver collar round each girl's neck chain. Like the girl I had seen running behind the farmer's cart, each girl's wrists were linked by another chain.

Each girl was holding an elaborate parasol, which she was trying to hold up over the bearded man's head to shield him from the sun.

The youths paid no attention to the scantily clad young women, although they were pretty things with large breasts, fine waists and swelling hips. It was as if the youths were used to seeing half naked girls running at the stirrup of the bearded man.

Suddenly one of the young women stumbled. The umbrella waived in the air, and hit one of the youths, who called out angrily to the bearded man, pointing disparagingly to the unfortunate girl who was now desperately trying to restore the parasol to its place above the bearded man.

The bearded man turned and said something to the Negro. The Negro rode his horse up behind the girl, who gave a terrified glance behind her. The Negro raised his whip and brought it down twice across the girl's back. She gave a little whimper, but continued to run on by the side of the horse, holding up her parasol.

The youth smiled at his companions and the cavalcade rode on, leaving me shocked at the scene that I had just witnessed.

Who were these youths? I remembered what the odious Irish Bey had said in Malta about wealthy men owning captured Christian slave girls and being accompanied by their white page-boys, 'garzons' he had said they were called. Clearly the youths were jealous of the girls. Presumably the Negro was the girl's overseer - I remembered what the Bey had said about his own black eunuchs beating a girl who had displeased him.

It was all very frightening. I had never seen women being treated with such callous cruelty.

Soon it was late afternoon. I had not eaten all day, and was becoming ravenously hungry. I crept back to the stream to drink, and was just returning to my hide-out when I saw a long four wheeled waggon drawn by two pairs of oxen coming round the corner of the track.

An Arab driver with a long whip was walking alongside the lumbering oxen urging them on. In front of the waggon was a large canvas awning, sheltering two other men. One was an Arab armed with a musket who seemed to be a guard.

The other man was a huge Negro wearing a white conical hat similar to those that I had seen before being worn by rather effeminate looking white youths like the Bey's 'garzon'. But there was nothing effeminate about this huge Negro - he was naked to the waist, his powerful torso shining in the evening sunlight, a whip in his hand, a whip that had a short handle and a short thick black flat leash.

But it was what I saw behind the awning that once again made me gasp in sheer disbelief. A raised metal bar ran down the middle of the waggon. Free to slide up and down the bar were some twenty metal rings. The bar was supported at either end of the waggon by wooden cross-pieces that held it several feet above the floor, and at either end of the bar were some sort of locked projections that would prevent the rings from sliding off, even if it were no longer supported by the cross-pieces. From each ring hung a length of stout chain, at the end of each chain was an iron collar, and each collar was fastened round the neck of a naked woman!

Some twenty women were sitting on the floor of the waggon in two lines facing each other. They were half hidden by its sides but exposed to the elements. I saw that they were nervously looking at each other and at the Negro in the front, but they did not talk to each other.

They were about to stop - the driver led the waggon just off the track and halted the oxen, and the Arab guard and the Negro climbed down from the waggon. They helped the driver to unhitch the oxen and to tether them nearby, giving them both water and a feed from sacks hanging under the waggon. Then they started to erect a tent and to build a fire, evidently preparing to camp for the night.

With my heart in my mouth for fear of being detected, I lay in my hide-out, watching them. Soon the aroma of meat being roasted drifted up to me, reminding me sharply of my own hunger. I began to lick my lips and to wonder if I could slip down later and steal some food.

Evidently the lamb being roasted on a spit was not for the women chained in the back of the waggon. I saw the powerful looking Negro go to the waggon and unhook a sack hanging from under it. He poured some of the contents into a large metal bowl - it looked like oats or barley. He added hot water from a large kettle boiling over the fire, and stirred the mixture until a sort of porridge had been formed.

Then he climbed up into the waggon and threw a dollop of the porridge onto the floor in front of each woman. I saw several fights break out as those who had finished their own rations quickly began to help themselves to those of their slower eating neighbours. The Negro laughed at their antics.

I was overcome at the cruel and barbarous way in which these white women were being treated, and by the way they had been reduced to the level of animals, fighting over their food.

I remembered what the hateful Bey had said about his black eunuchs disciplining the women in his harem. Was this massive brute a black eunuch? Was that why he wore that strange conical hat? But if so, then why had the youths I had seen earlier on also worn it? Surely not even the Turks and Moors would make eunuchs out of captured Christian boys? Or was that why they had seemed so soft skinned - like little boys?

But who were the women in the waggon? Why were they chained and naked? Where were they being taken?

Chapter 2

CAPTURED

I crept through the darkness down towards the waggon.

I could hear the clinking of chains as the women stirred, and laughter coming from the tent where the men were eating. Two of the men's voices were deep, but one was curiously high pitched. There were no voices coming from the waggon.

I reached the track at the bottom of the small hill. At last the waggon containing the women was in front of me, close, silent.

I looked round, then drew breath.

"Hullo there - don't make a noise," I whispered in Lingua Franca, the mixture of basic Italian and Spanish that was widely used throughout the Mediterranean, and which I had learnt in Sicily.

There was a sudden movement of chains. "Who's there?" called out a woman, frightened.

"Shush!" I whispered urgently. "Be quiet, please! I'm a friend."

"What's going on?" whispered another woman. I heard the movement of more chains, of bodies.

I climbed up over the side of the waggon and quickly lowered myself to the floor beside the captive women. It was covered with straw on which they were lying, their collar chains fastened to the metal pole that ran the length of the waggon above them. There was hardly any room to move. I felt naked female flesh, soft and yielding.

Quickly I squeezed in to lie down amongst them. I could not risk being seen.

"Who are you? ... What do you want?"

"Shush! Please keep quiet," I whispered.

"Who are you?"

"I'm Barbara. I'm Irish. From Malta. I've been shipwrecked and I need help."

"How can we help? ... We're chained ... We're slaves," a voice replied. "We've only just been captured ourselves ..."

"Give me some food," I begged.

"We have no food! We just have to scramble for what is thrown to us."

I moaned in my distress. "But the food being cooked by the men ..."

"That's not for us!"

"But, please, please, you must help me!" I cried.

"What can we do?" came a new voice. "We are kept chained like animals."

Again there was a pause. "Are you a runaway slave? ... Have you escaped from your Master?" The voices suddenly became urgent, almost hysterical. "How did you do it? ... Where will you go? ... Can you cut free our chains?... Can you take us with you?"

"No, no, you don't understand. I'm not a slave. I tell you I have been shipwrecked. I'm an Irishwoman, from Malta. I'm not a slave."

"Well you soon will be, you little fool." There was laughter.

A girl seized my left arm. She held it so that the light from the men's camp fire lit it up through a gap in the planking in the side of the waggon. I felt my arm being turned.

"It's true what she says. She's got no number."

"What do you mean?" I whispered, snatching away my arm.

"Look! Look at my arm," said the girl.

18

In the half light I could make out that something strange had indeed been tattooed along the soft skin inside her forearm.

"Arabic numerals," explained the girl. "My slave number - registered at the port at which we were disembarked: somewhere near Tunis, we think it was."

"Yes," came another voice, bitterly, "not only are we kept chained like animals, and fed like animals, but we have even been tattooed with a number so that our Masters can keep a record of us - just like my father used to record his live-stock on our farm ... You must go quickly. You must get away from here!"

"But where to?" I moaned piteously. "I don't even know where I am! Where do I go to get help? Where can I get some food?"

"Not here, that's for sure!"

"Nowhere on the Barbary Coast!"

"It's too late now! The Negro's coming for Slave Check!"

I saw a lantern coming towards the waggon. I heard the crack of a whip and a high pitched voice, shouting in broken Lingua Franca.

"Animals! No talking!"

My arm was suddenly gripped by one of the women. "Quick, you fool, take off your shift so that you're naked like us. Hide it in the straw. And put this collar round your neck. It doesn't matter that you can't lock it. It's from a girl who died two days ago."

"Died?" I whispered anxiously as she put the collar round my neck. It was hinged at one side, with two flanges meeting on the other, through which a padlock or rivet could be fitted.

"Yes. Perhaps being enslaved was all too much for her. Who knows? Oh do hurry! He's coming! Quick! Lie down here and just hope that he doesn't notice you."

I heard the heavy footsteps of the big Negro coming closer, and lay flat on the floor like all the other women.

I put my hands over my face, partly to hide it, and partly to hold the collar shut. I could feel the weight not only of the iron collar itself, but also of the thick chain that linked it to the metal bar over us. It made me feel helpless, as I suppose it was intended to do.

I heard the whip crack again. I felt the women on either side of me flinch. It was terrifying. I now understood for the first time the power that a ruthless man with a whip can have over a woman - particularly a naked one. The fact that the man was a burly Negro, and I a delicate white woman, made it all the more terrifying. I half closed my eyes in fear, lying curled up on my side.

The back of the waggon was let down. I felt it sway under the weight of the huge Negro as he stepped up into it. Several women moaned, more in fear than in pain, as he kicked them out of his way. He was coming up towards me! Petrified, I lay absolutely still.

A few seconds later I glimpsed the naked and muscular torso of the eunuch as he stood over me, holding up his lantern. He was wearing baggy Turkish breeches, or shalwar, that came down to his calves. I saw his cunning beady eyes, the frightening tribal scars on his cheeks.

He was looking down at the woman alongside me. then his eyes switched to me and flickered over my head, then travelled on down my naked body.

He had not noticed that my collar was not properly fastened round my neck, nor that the dead girl's empty collar was now missing. Suddenly his eyes rested on my belly and stopped. With his foot he kicked me over onto my back.

"So an unshorn little animal has come to join us!" he said in his high falsetto voice. It seemed odd, such a high pitched voice coming from such a burly body. He began to laugh. Suddenly he snatched at the chain leading down to my collar, wrenching it out of my hands.

"So Allah the merciful, Allah the provider, has sent me a new slave to replace the dead one!"

He turned and shouted at his two companions, still by the fireside, and they came running.

I heard expressions of astonishment, then one of them handed something, like a huge pair of pliers with wooden handles, up to the Negro. It must have been what he had called to them to bring. I cringed as he bent down over me.

"No, please, please ..." I begged.

He paid no attention. He put the collar back round my neck. Then he inserted something into the two flanges that met on the side of my neck opposite to the hinge. It was a lead pellet. He put down his whip and handed the lantern to one of the men. Holding the huge pliers in both hands, he put it down onto my collar. Suddenly he squeezed the two handles together with a grunt, squeezing the leaden pellet into the flanges. The collar was now riveted round my neck. I was chained, like the other women, to the long iron bar above me.

The Negro laughed. "That animal won't escape now," he muttered in Lingua Franca to himself. "Unless it dies like the other one!"

He stood up and handed the rivet squeezer back to his companions, and took back the lantern. He reached down and grabbed my left arm, and turned it over. He grunted when he saw no tattooed number. He called out something in Arabic to the two men, making them laugh.

He reached down to my belly. "Belly up!" he screamed. "Raise right up, when I give you order."

Terrified I raised myself to him, just as I had seen the other girl do. When he touched me, I gave a little cry. He paid no attention. He was feeling my body hair.

"You!" he said. "Tomorrow I take all off. Tomorrow you smooth like the others. Tomorrow you tattooed with number of dead girl."

I heard one of the Arabs rummaging in the front of the waggon. He came back holding a sheet of paper covered in Arabic writing, and began to read it aloud. The eunuch

21

held up his lantern to my head and touched my hair. Apparently satisfied, he nodded.

I realised that the paper must be the manifest for the load of women slaves. He must be comparing me with the brief description of the dead girl. Presumably he would be blamed for her death, for arriving with one girl less than on the manifest. But if he replaced her with me, and if I fitted her description and bore her registered slave number, then no one need ever know about the death of the girl. It was lucky for him that I had dark hair!

Then the man with the list read out something else in Arabic. The Negro looked down at me. "You virgin?"

His eyes were on my raised belly. I was too embarrassed, too scared, to be able to speak. Suddenly he brought the thick leather blade of his whip down across my belly. It was as if a live coal had been dropped onto it. The pain took my breath away. I had never felt anything like it. I screamed in agony.

"Virgin?" he queried, raising his whip again. "You virgin?"

"Yes! Yes!" I shouted.

The big Negro smiled and said something to his companions. Then he turned back to me.

"I check. Get over!" With his boot he rolled me over on onto my stomach. "Kneel up on all fours! Head down! Knees wider apart! Thrust bottom back! More! Now you keep quite still. You move, you get whip again. Understand?"

Kneeling on all fours like an animal on the crowded floor of the waggon I suddenly felt his hand. I jumped. My collar chain rattled. "Oh!" I cried. "Oh!" I sobbed. No man had ever touched me there before.

"Keep still, you Christian dog," the Negro growled menacingly, as he parted my body lips. I felt him beginning to probe. For the first time in my life my virginity was being checked. I could feel him exploring carefully. I was overcome with shame. Then his finger was withdrawn, He stood up.

"Good!" he said. "You now slave number 875632."

"No! No!" I cried. "You've made a mistake. A terrible mistake. I'm not a slave. I'm Miss Barbara Kennedy. I'm a British subject. I've been shipwrecked. I'm not a slave ..."

"Slave now," came the angry reply. He raised the terrifying whip menacingly. He consulted the paper again. "You slave number 875632, virgin, captured in raid on Italian coast. Tomorrow I tattoo you with number. You understand?"

I nodded, my eyes on the terrible thick hide whip. I did indeed understand. Miss Barbara Kennedy, a well educated and respectable young Irish governess had simply disappeared off the face of the earth. In her place was now Slave Number 875632, with black hair, a virgin, captured in a raid on the Italian coast.

There was no official record that I was British. The treaties between Britain and the various Barbary States, exempting British subjects from slavery, would not apply to me, even if they were worth the paper they were written on.

Would I ever see the green hills of Ireland again? Would I ever see my precious Dermot again?

Chapter 3

MY FIRST TASTE OF SLAVERY

True to his word, early the following morning the Negro, huge, hideous and bald, strapped my arm to the side of the waggon. Then very carefully, he tattooed Arabic numbers onto the inside of my left forearm.

The sight made me feel that I really was now a slave.

I had to learn, as the other women had already learned, that on the command 'Present!' I must kneel up, hold out my arm out straight, palm upwards and exactly level with my navel, and show my slave number. At the same time I had to clasp my other hand behind my neck, put out my tongue, look straight ahead and part my knees wide. It was a humiliating position, intended to show off a slave's submissiveness.

"Now you slave! Just like the other women. Slave of Hassan Ali, your Master," the Negro said approvingly in his heavily accented Lingua Franca. "I take you all to him."

So we had a Master: Hassan Ali! Who he was, and where he lived, the Negro did not tell us. When one woman asked, she was beaten, beaten hard by our black overseer. "Slaves not ask questions!" he said slowly, punctuating each word with another stroke of his whip.

This was just after he had made me practice over and over the degrading position of 'Present'.

"You forget past life," the Negro said as he finished tattooing me with my slave number. "You now just slave number 875632. Slaves not use Christian names. Until new Master give you new name, you just '632'. What your name, girl?"

"632!" I replied. I was kneeling naked in front of him. Angrily he raised his whip, that terrible whip with it's thick leather blade.

"Sir!" I added quickly, overcome by sheer fear. "632, Sir!"

"That better," the huge Negro muttered. "Now you remember, you only do what I, Bashir Aga, the Beater of Slave Women, say to do."

"Oh!" I exclaimed, shocked. But at least I had learned the name of my terrifying overseer.

How could I, Miss Barbara Kennedy, a strong minded and independent Irish girl, have been reduced to such a state? By the whip! By the whip! It was all too awful.

That morning he also started to depilate me. Like all the other women I was kneeling in line on one side of the waggon, in the shameful position of "Present". Bashir Aga came down the line carrying a large pot of some sort of cream. As he passed each girl, he bent down and smeared her beauty lips with the cream. When he came to me, I longed to lower my hands to protect my intimacies, to cry out in protest, to look down to see what he was doing, and to press my thighs close together. But I did not dare do any of these. Such is the power of a man with a whip!

Still looking straight ahead I felt him rub the cream into my body hair and then down along my body lips. It was too awful! Finally, he moved onto the next girl. Suddenly I felt a growing burning sensation between my thighs. I wanted to cry out, but I did dare to do so. The burning sensation grew worse. I lowered my hands to brush away the awful cream, but the Negro was onto me like a shot, as if he had just been waiting for such a reaction.

"Get hands back!" he screamed, giving me a stroke of his whip across my breasts. "You let cream be, not look down!"

For a full five minutes I had to kneel up, biting my lips whilst the cream did its work. Then the pain began to wear off a little.

When the Negro repeated the process on the line of women facing me across the floor of the waggon, I could see that they only suffered pain for the first minute or so, presumably because they were already smooth and hairless. The Negro would run his hand over each woman's mound and down her lips, as if feeling for any remaining stubble or hairs, and then rub the cream in accordingly.

To be treated in this degrading way by a Negro was almost more than I could bear! But it was to be part of my daily early morning routine. Soon I was as smooth and hairless as the rest of the women. "Just like baby girl!" said Bashir Aga approvingly, as he ran his hand down my parted beauty lips. "That how Arab men like see Christian slave woman."

Christian slave woman! I remembered how the awful Bey had said that he had Christian slave women in his harem. Did he have them depilated too? Had he been looking at me, wondering what I would look like with hairless beauty lips? Oh what a shameful thought! What a dreadful man he was. But, well - if only he were here to rescue me and send me back to Malta!

I found myself settling down to the degrading morning routine. At dawn we would be awoken by the noise of our overseer striking his whip against the side of the waggon. Instantly we would all kneel up in the position of 'Present', calling out our slave numbers for him to tick off

26

against his list, whilst we held out our forearms for him to check the numbers.

Then with our hands now clasped behind our necks and not daring to look down, we had to endure the burning depilatory cream. Not only did it remove all signs of body hair, I noticed, but it also gradually seemed to stop the hair from growing back.

Then the Negro would unfasten the long metal bar to which our collar chains were attached. Lifting it up and jumping down carefully from the waggon, we had to form up in two lines again facing each other. A locked projection at either end of the bar prevented the rings at the end of our collar chains from slipping off the end of the bar. We still remained attached to the heavy bar, which we were now carrying.

At a word of command from the Negro, assisted by a fearsome crack of his whip, my line of women had to take the entire weight of the bar. Holding it up high above heads, with our legs wide apart, we then had to bend our knees. We were now in an awkward squatting position, the Negro walking up and down behind us.

Suddenly there would come another crack of the whip from behind us. It was the signal to get ready to perform. We were just like a team of well trained performing animals. When the whip cracked again, the Negro would expect to see ten little fountains instantly splashing onto the sandy ground. Woebetide any girl who was even a few seconds late in starting - the whip would descend twice across her back! At first I simply could not perform to order like that in front of the Negro. But, by God, I soon learned to do so.

I wondered how I would look any man in the face after what I was being made to do here - and certainly not my betrothed, Dermot.

Another crack of the whip was the signal for us to stop instantly, whether we had finished or not, to stand up and to pass the heavy bar to the line facing us. It was now their turn to perform onto the sand.

Our iron collars fitted loosely round our necks. At a word of command, therefore, an entire line was able to turn round, still holding the iron bar high up above its heads, so that both lines were now facing the same way, with the front rank holding up the bar, to which of course the second rank were still attached by their collar chains.

At a crack of the whip we would set off, at a smart trot, running round and round the waggon. We had to run in perfect step, raising our knees high in the air. It was tiring enough for the second rank who were just running in this exaggerated prancing fashion. For the first rank, who were also holding the heavy bar up above their heads, it was utterly exhausting.

At last the whip would crack again - the signal for both ranks to halt and for the front rank to turn about. Then at another crack of the whip they had to hand the bar to the second rank, who at a further crack of the whip had to turn about smartly, so that they then became the front rank. Then we would all have to prance round and round the waggon again, this time going the other way round.

The whole exhausting process would be repeated over and over again.

Like performing animals in a circus, we had to learn to carry out the routine to the crack of the whip with hardly any orders being given. I suppose it was a way of breaking us in to our slavery and of keeping us on our toes, with the ever present threat of the whip ready to punish any girl who made the slightest mistake.

Bashir Aga certainly knew all about exercising women's bodies. I could feel my whole body becoming fitter and slimmer as I sweated and pranced round the wretched waggon, half the time holding up that heavy bar with every muscle in my body crying out for relief. I could feel my bouncing breasts becoming firmer by the day, and even larger.

Bashir Aga also seemed to have an uncanny way of knowing when an exhausted girl was only pretending to help hold the heavy bar up high. In my early days, I often felt the whip across my back. I learnt to fear and hate Bashir Aga. His muscles rippling, he would take a devilish delight in applying his whip so that the tip would flick round under my uplifted arms and catch my tender breasts.

It was a simple and yet very effective way of both exercising our bodies and instilling discipline. It was also one that was not made more enjoyable by the catcalls of the inevitable small crowd of Arab children, who had come from the nearest village to watch the hated Christian women being put through their paces. To be drilled by a black overseer whilst stark naked in front of jeering Arab children was very degrading.

But worse would follow.

By now several older Arab peasants would usually have joined the jeering children. They and the Negro would start bargaining. A deal having been struck, he would make us empty ourselves in turn into a brass bowl, the contents of which we had to mix up with the wastes of the oxen. It was all carefully weighed and sold to the peasants. Evidently the revolting mixture was much sought after to fertilise their small holdings. Woebetide, once again, any girl who did not contribute instantly to our overseer's earnings. As I myself learnt to my cost, any hesitation resulted in an immediate large dose of castor oil.

By now the oxen would have been fed, watered and hitched up again to the waggon. We would then have to carry the bar back into the waggon. Then we would take up our places again on the straw covered floor, our backs to the side of the waggon, and our heavy collar chains still fastened to the bar now back in its place overhead.

Talking was only allowed for two short periods of the day. "Animals don't talk!" was a favourite expression of

29

our eunuch whipmaster. How eagerly we would await each precious talking session, planning ahead in silence what we would say to our neighbours.

It was strictly forbidden to use our Christian names or surnames. We had to use the last three figures of our slave number. So I was "632". Soon I learned to answer to my number. But in fact we used to whisper our names to each other, even if officially we had to call each other by our numbers.

We were also forbidden to talk about our life before we were captured, but one day, when the Negro was out of earshot, my friendly neighbour, Carlotta, whispered to me that she had just been married when one night the corsairs had landed on the coast nearby and raided the village, where they had settled, carrying off all the younger women and all the boys.

"And now," she whispered with a sob, "... I'm carrying my husband's child ... and he'll never know. But that pig of a black eunuch, he knows alright! He misses nothing when it comes to a woman. He says it will put up my value when we are sold."

"Sold where?" I asked.

"We don't know, but it seems that Hassan Ali is a slave dealer. We are just his latest consignment to be trained ready for the market. But change the subject, the Negro is coming back."

Later I spoke to the slightly older woman chained on my other side. She had the air of a lady, despite her nakedness. She whispered that she was a Condessa from Tuscany, captured with her daughter who was the pretty young girl chained opposite us. She had gone to visit her daughter who was at a convent school by the sea, when in the middle of the night corsairs had broken in. They had seized every personable young woman, and even two of the younger nuns.

"Perhaps my husband's family will ransom us," she kept saying. "But they will demand such a huge one that it will ruin the family."

Pay a ransom! No one would have the money to pay a huge ransom for me, I thought bitterly, even if they did somehow learn that I was a slave girl in Barbary.

At first the waggon had been moving across rocky wild countryside. Now, however, it was becoming increasingly cultivated and more highly populated. The drivers would frequently stop to gossip with the men in the villages. The women were normally hidden by all enveloping long shrouds. They incorporated a small piece of lace that went in front of the eyes, and through which the women could see a little, without being seen. Only out in the real country did the women go unveiled, and even then, free women would hastily veil themselves as we approached.

The contrast between these veiled women, and us slaves, chained and naked, was bitter. Even so I noticed that, veiled as they were, they still carried anything heavy or dirty for their menfolk, as they walked dutifully behind them. Evidently here men did not demean themselves with physical effort. That was left to women.

The squalor and filth in the villages was appalling. But there seemed little real poverty. I was astonished how little interest the passing of a waggon loaded with twenty naked white women seemed to arouse. It was as if such a sight was commonplace. Indeed we passed several waggons like ours going northwards with loads of cotton and woollen goods. Would they soon be returning with another load of white women?

It was with a shock of horror that, as we passed a large estate, I first saw a team of half naked white women, harnessed to the plough and straining under the whip of the ploughman. White women cost as little to feed as oxen I suppose, and were probably easier to control - with the whip! Several, I was shocked to see, were pregnant!

Other teams of women, sometimes all white and sometimes mixed with brown mulattoes, were being driven round and round a threshing yard, sweating and straining as they hauled round a flat platform on which stood a Negro overseer, whip in hand.

I also saw pairs of white women, often it seemed carefully matched, being made to run round a well, harnessed to a heavy beam that turned the screw that, in turn, brought up the water and discharged it into rivulets which irrigated the land. Sometimes animals were used, donkeys, camels or oxen, and sometimes a mixture of women and animals.

Shocked and horrified, I fervently hoped that I would not end up as a beast of burden on a farm - a mere field slave, like the Negro slaves in America and the West Indies. But they worked under the whip of white overseers. These women were working under the whip of black overseers. Were those with child pregnant by them? I was appalled. But was the alternative any better?

Chapter 4

HASSAN ALI'S ESTATE

At last it seemed that our long slow journey was over.

There was a feeling of excitement in the waggon and we kept trying to crane our chained necks over the sides. We were approaching a large Arab town. There were numerous small, but well irrigated, farms. Small fields of mint gave off an exquisite scent. I could see that there a port, well protected by a large landlocked bay. I could see the masts of ships. There was an air of prosperity about it all.

"Marsa", announced Bashir Aga.

Marsa!

Instead of going straight towards that infamous place, we were skirting it. Bashir Aga pointed to a large well kept estate, set on a hillside, and surrounded by a high wall. There were spikes on the top to make it even more difficult to get over. I wondered whether it was more intended to keep people out or to keep people or animals in.

"Listen, Christian dogs! This estate of your Master, Hassan Ali," he announced proudly.

We had imagined that Hassan Ali was simply a slave dealer, but evidently he was much more than that.

"He pay for Corso that capture you. You all part of his share of profits. He send me collect you."

At last the jigsaw was beginning to fall into place. No wonder the big Negro overseer had been so worried about

33

the girl who had died. Clearly Hassan Ali was a man power and substance. No wonder the Negro had been delighted to find me in her place.

Soon we passed through the gates of Hassan Ali's large estate. They were guarded by armed Negroes wearing bright red uniforms and red fez hats, and carrying muskets and whips.

They grinned at Bashir Aga, and pointing to us exchanged ribald remarks. I remembered my earlier thoughts about the white female field slaves on the farms apparently being regularly covered by their Negro overseers as I looked at these huge guards. Their voices were not the least bit falsetto!

Fields of cotton, maize, and vegetables were interspersed with groves of oranges, lemons, peaches, figs and olives. They were all carefully laid out and divided by well kept paths and carriageways. The land seemed much more fertile than the land outside the walls.

We passed large white buildings, designed to hold various animals: horses, oxen, donkeys and, I was soon to learn, women slaves.

A well dressed Negro overseer was walking up and down behind the girls seated at their looms, the inevitable whip in his hand. This must be why they were kept naked - to make it easier to use the whip on them if they slackened off, or gossiped to their neighbours instead of concentrating on their work.

Horrified, I saw that each woman was chained to her loom by a chain fastened to an iron collar riveted round her neck - just like mine. Mother of God! I thought, is that why we have been brought here? To be slaves in a carpet factory! I was even more horrified when I saw one of the girls stand up to adjust her loom. She was pregnant! Oh no, I thought, oh no!

Our cart moved on and I saw herds of goats, presumably kept for their milk like those of Malta, being led to what seemed to be a milking parlour. Coming out of it, under the supervision of a huge Negro carrying a whip, was a line of white women, chained together by their neck and stripped to the waist. Their breasts all seemed to be exceptionally large and covered in blue veins like those of women in milk. They looked at us with interest, but did not dare to speak. Surely. I thought, they could not really be some sort of human milk herd? Was the milk of white women regarded as a delicacy here in this barbaric land?

Then we passed groups of mares and foals, and in-foal mares, grazing contentedly in what were evidently well manured paddocks. By now it was clear to me that Hassan Ali was a man of considerable wealth.

The waggon moved on, and I saw a line of young white women, chained loosely by the neck to form a long line, hoeing a field under the supervision of yet another Negro with a whip. He looked as brutal as our Bashir Aga as he periodically cracked it, making his charges flinch and redouble their efforts. Might this be my fate? To be a field slave, a milk slave, or a factory girl in this terrifying place?

Another line of sturdy looking girls, perhaps peasant girls from Italy or Spain, and wearing short smocks, were laboriously taking a mixture of wet straw and manure from a cart and digging it into the ground.

Shortly afterwards we passed a chain of women with blond hair and blue eyes. They seemed very like one another. They reminded me of the Condessa and her daughter. Their fair colouring certainly made them conspicuous. I wondered where so many blonde women had come from. Blonde women were rare in the Mediterranean. Although still chained like the other women, they were dressed in pretty dark blue tunics with a crest of crossed scimitars, presumably the crest of Hassan Ali, embroidered on the breast.

Clearly they were regarded as exceptionally valuable slaves and not used for labouring. I saw that their black overseer, unlike the others I had seen, wore the pointed cap that was, it seemed, the badge of a eunuch.

The black eunuch was making each of them take off her tunic before being made to crawl back naked into one of a line of low straw lined cages. Presumably this was to prevent their tunics from getting soiled as the women crawled round the crowded cage, which was only about three feet high.

Suddenly I realised why the whole estate seemed so fertile. By keeping his women slaves in cages, Hassan Ali was able to use their wastes, already trampled into the straw, to supplement that of his farm animals, in providing a source of first class fertiliser. Even the pampered blonde women had to provide their wastes for the estate. It was all so devilishly callous - but clever.

The eunuch was writing in a notebook as a blonde woman shyly presented her swollen belly, breasts and beauty lips for his inspection

I saw that many of these blonde women were pregnant, and they were allowed to keep a little tuft of blond hair on one side - presumably to prove that they really were blond.

Then I saw that the cages at the end of the line held men. In one was a white man with a blond beard! Scandinavian? He was naked except for a sort of metal pouch which was locked round his loins. There were holes to allow the passage of liquids wastes but he would be unable to touch his manhood.

In the next door cage was a little black pygmy, anxiously gripping the bars of his cage and looking at us eagerly and licking his lips.

Another Negro was leading a dark haired white girl up to the his cage. She too was screaming and crying, but she too helpless with her hands tied behind her. Grinning, the Negro pushed her into the cage.

Then our waggon passed on and I could see nothing more. Like the other women in the waggon, I was shaking with fear at what I had seen. We did not dare talk about it, however.

I tried to make out the significance of what I had seen. Did their hatred for us Christians made them feel morally justified in treating poor girls like us as animals, to be used for labouring and breeding, just like other domestic animals? Were dark haired girls mated with their Negro overseers or with the pygmy? Were they used to produce little mulattoes to be sold as work slaves, or dwarfs to be sold as playthings?

Clearly, the chain of blonde women were treated quite differently. They seemed to• have a black eunuch in charge of them, presumably to ensure that they only became pregnant by the blond male captive.

I supposed that many of them, being blond, had themselves been bred in the cages and kept back for further breeding, knowing no other life. Presumably, also, the blond man had been captured from a ship and was used as a stallion on all the blonde women, both the few who had themselves been captured and those who had been specially bred. The price for blonde women, I realised, must be far higher than that for typical dark haired Mediterranean girls - or dark haired Irish colleens, I thought ruefully.

Approaching the inlet was a small galley with perhaps ten oars a side. I had never seen a galley before. I could just make out the galley slaves straining at their oars on the open benches, and a figure reclining in comfort in the covered raised poop. The galley was flying several green flags, marked with the crescent. Clearly it was bringing someone important to Hassan Ali's estate ...

Chapter 5

PREPARATIONS FOR INSPECTION

Our waggon finally came to a halt in front of a fine looking Arab style building.

The back of the waggon was let down. The heavy bar, along which ran the rings to which our collar chains were secured, was unfastened from the two cross-pieces that had held it above our heads. Bashir Aga curtly ordered us to lift up the bar and to jump down one at a time from the waggon. As before, locked projections at the end of the ends of the bar to which we were chained prevented the rings from slipping off.

Just as we had done every morning, we formed up into two lines, one holding up the bar, the other standing behind the first one. We were led inside, our heavy chains rattling and clinking as we moved, and found ourselves in a pretty room with mirrors on the wall. In the centre was a large bath, and on shelves round the room were brushes, combs, creams, rouges and powder.

Our overseer ordered us to lay the bar down alongside the bath. Still chained to it, we gratefully slid into the bath and began to wash off the dust and grime of the journey. For the first time since I had been chained to that accursed bar, I began to feel like a woman again.

It was indeed wonderful to lather myself all over with soap - an experience marred only by having to do it under the close direction of a black eunuch. Then, one at a time, we had to crawl out of the bath and stand, our legs

wide apart, in front of the now seated Negro, and then
turn round and touch our toes, whilst he inspected us
carefully to ensure that we were meticulously clean.

We were being prepared for - what?

Then, again under the direction of our whipmaster,
we had to dry our hair and brush it until it shone, heavily
rouge our cheeks, and powder our bodies all over.
Standing in front of a mirror, and looking at my naked
body, I was shocked at the sight of my depilated body lips.
Our overseer's constant application of that burning
cream had done its work well. There was not a sign of a
hair anywhere. My most secret intimacies were now well
displayed, and the the effect when I parted my legs was
shame-making to a girl who had been brought up in a
convent.

My belly was now more rounded and softer - thanks
to the horrible slave gruel. I also saw that my breasts
were firmer and fuller, thanks to the awful exercises with
the heavy bar.

Looking around I saw that all the women were admiring
themselves in the mirrors and titivating themselves. We
were all looking good, and this cheered us enormously,
even if we were still stark naked.

Even Bashir Aga was grinning broadly.

"Perhaps little Christian girls like permission for
talkie-talkie?" he asked. We nodded eagerly. It was
humiliating being talked to as if we were little children,
but it was better than being treated as mere animals.

Soon the room was full of the chatter of twenty
attractive women, all laughing and giggling like school
girls. It was hard to believe that only a week or two before
I had been a strict governess in the employ an Ambassador.

We made up each other's eyes and brushed each
other's hair. It was wonderful to look pretty again. Our
eyes sparkled. We told each other how lovely we looked.
Somehow I felt that even my heavy neck chain made feel

and look more feminine, more desirable, in a way that no governess had ever felt nor looked.

Suddenly Bashir Aga clapped his hands, and looked grim again. "Your Master, Hassan Ali, he coming soon to see new slaves. No more talking!"

He made us pick up the heavy bar and led us through into a beautiful and spacious room. The floor was tiled with shiny marble and the windows were covered with arabesque lattice tracery through which a cool breeze entered. Along one side of the room was a prominently raised dais with sumptuous cushions and Turkish style sofas. In front of them were small carved tables laden with Turkish Delight and other tantalising sweetmeats. Not for us!

We had to place the bar onto little supports. It was now at right angles to the dais. We were lined up in our usual two lines, this time facing each other and the bar, as we had been in the waggon, our heavy chains hanging down between our breasts and leading up to the bar. Anyone on the platform would get a sideways look at our bodies. I felt like a performing dog on a lead.

"Down on hands and knees!" The Negro cracked his whip. I could not help trembling. "Palms flat on floor! Fingers together! Heads up! Look straight ahead!"

Our overseer was walking up and down behind my line of kneeling women. I did not dare turn round to look at him. Suddenly, with a crack, he brought his whip down onto the marble floor. We were all now very frightened and desperately anxious to obey him.

"Keep backs straight! Let breasts hang down for Master to see! Get bottoms up higher! Higher! Arms straight! Suck in bellies! Eyes fixed ahead!"

I strained to arch my back and to raise my head and my buttocks.

"You! 632!" I jumped as I heard my number being called. He touched me with his whip. I was shivering with fear. "Knees wider apart! Wider!" It was a shameful position, especially now that I had been depilated.

"Remember you going to be inspected by man. What you do?"

"Open our legs wide, Sir!" we chorused. We had already learned this basic lesson well.

"Good! Now when Master, Master's friends and Master's managers enter room to inspect new slaves, I want you standing still in two lines, heads up, hands clasped behind neck, eyes looking straight ahead, legs wide apart. Then, when they all sit down, I clap hands. You all fall to knees. Go onto all fours like now, but you put forehead to floor, palms of hands flat on floor on either side of head. Slaves stay down until I order 'Heads up!'. Then raise only heads. You stay on all fours, like now. Above all you look ahead. You not dare look at Master. You understand?"

"Yes, Sir," we chorused.

"Then I call slave number of woman at end of bar nearest Master."

He paused. He looked around to make sure we were all paying attention.

"I unlock ring of neck chain from end of bar and lead slave up to foot of dais.

"Then I crack whip, you crawl to master, lick shoes take robe in both hands. You kiss robe, like he God."

"After each woman led away to start new life, slaves all move up one place towards dais. Not speak, unless spoken to. Master only interested in decide what to do with your body, not your mind. Remember all time whip waiting. Waiting for you!" Again he brought it down with a terrifying crash onto the marble floor. "What you say?"

"Please, Sir, spare me the whip! I will be humble and obedient!" we all chorused. He had drilled us well during the long journey.

"Now pay careful attention! When I say 'Up!', you sit up. You spread knees wide. You clasp hands behind neck. You thrust breast forwards. You show yourself off to Master, he decide how best use you."

It sounded very degrading, but worse was to follow. What did he mean, I wondered, about how we were to be used? I remembered the sight of the field slaves, of the girls in the carpet factory and of the milk slaves, and shivered.

"Then when I say 'Stand up!' you jump up, stand up straight, at attention, legs together, hands still behind neck, still looking straight ahead."

It was all too awful!

"Then Master discuss how best use you with Master of Field Slaves, with Master of Milk Slaves, with Master of Carpet Factory, with Animal Breeding Master, with Head Trainer of Brothel Slaves, with Trainer of Harem Slaves. May be if Dairy Master interested, he order you to crawl round to judge hang of breasts."

Field Slaves! Milk Slaves! Animal Breeding! Brothel Slaves! Harem Slaves! And I was about to be chosen for one of these! I scarcely knew which was worst. Then my convent training took over. To be a slave in a brothel, used by different men, would be far worse than anything else.

"Now we practice!"

And practice we did: over and over again, kneeling in abject obeisance, our heads to floor, crawling up to the dais, jumping up to stand at attention. I was really getting a foretaste of what it was going to be like to be a white slave in Barbary.

Suddenly there was the noise of men arriving outside. In a few minutes, I thought, my fate will be decided. I was scared stiff, paralysed with fear, my eyes fixed ahead.

Footsteps and deep male voices. To my shame, I could feel myself being aroused by the sound and the excitement.

The men were chatting and laughing as they swept past us up to the dais. They did not even seem to notice our presence. I was vaguely aware, out of the corner of my eye, of beautiful Moorish slippers, of spotless robes, of graceful gestures, of Eastern courtesy, of cultured male charm, of white page boys carrying fans, of the clink of porcelain coffee cups, and of cut glass goblets ...

The contrast between all that and us naked, cringing, chained women, was devastating. These were indeed Gods, men to be worshipped by us mere slave women. We were like dust at their feet. We were just animals for them to use as they best decided.

I heard them sit down on the dais. Greatly daring I very slightly turned my head, hoping that the Negro would not notice. Through my fingers, I glanced very briefly up at the dais, before lowering my eyes back to the floor. I had seen, sitting in the middle, a vastly fat, stern looking, grey bearded, man. Hassan Ali, my owner!

Two page boys were standing behind him, fanning his sweating jowls. Two more were kneeling at his feet, looking up at him, and rubbing his ankles. They had been pretty European boys with painted girlish eyes and soft skins. My owner had been stroking their long hair absent-mindedly. Clearly, I thought, the hair of these boy slaves was not cut off and sold - unlike that of many of his slave girls. I felt a surge of jealousy. Clearly my Master liked boys, gelded like the Bey's page boy.

The Negro clapped his hands. I was so overcome with fear that for a moment I forgot all that we had been practising. There was little left in me in me of the fiery, independent young Irish woman I had once been.

"Down!" hissed the Negro. I saw that he was bowing deeply.

I fell to my knees alongside the other women. I opened my legs wide and raised my bottom, I straightened and arched my back, utterly degraded. I was the lowest of the low, a naked Christian slave girl. My still unknown Master and his companions, and even their Negro overseers, nominally slaves like me, were infinitely superior. They were like Gods!

Then greatly daring, I then took another quick peek up at the dais. Surrounding the revoltingly fat figure of Hassan Ali was a group of well dressed Arabs in flowing jelabas, presumably the managers of his various enterprises. Angrily I wondered which were the swine in charge of using helpless white women to be bred against their will for the greater profit of Hassan Ali. Which, I wanted to scream, was the pig in charge of forcing respectable Christian girls into being trained as whores for luxury brothels? Which was responsible for training field slaves and for apparently making them produce an annual crop of carefully bred mulatto children? Which was responsible for the production of the highly valuable blond children?

Suddenly I felt my heart jump.

It couldn't be true! I took another careful peek.

There sitting up on the dais, and being fanned by a page boy, who looked remarkably like Tulip, was a man remarkably like ... quite remarkably like ... was indeed the handsome and arrogant Irish Bey, Rory Fitzgerald, whose face I had publicly smacked in Malta!

It couldn't be!

But it was! It was indeed he, the Bey. And the page boy was indeed Tulip.

I almost fainted with excitement.

Thank the good Lord, rescue was at hand!

Forgetting everything I had been made to practice by Bashir Aga, I raised my head and looked towards the dais. I was frightened that the Bey would not recognise me. The naked woman now kneeling before him with her hair hanging down her back, must seem very different from the well dressed and well groomed Irish governess, her hair swept up, whom he had briefly met at the Ball in Malta only a short before.

But he would recognise me even so.

I called out in English.

"Sir! Sir! It's me, Barbara, Barbara Kennedy!"

Chapter 6

THE SELECTION

I was about to launch into a long account of the shipwreck and of how I had been enslaved by that swine Bashir Aga, when suddenly his whip flashed down across my bare back.

I screamed with pain. It was as if I had suddenly been burnt with a red hot poker. The whip flashed down again.

As my outburst had been in English no one except the Bey could have understood it, but clearly the Negro eunuch felt that he had been ridiculed in front of his Master. He was livid with rage. I had given Hassan Ali the impression that he, Bashir Aga, the Beater of Women, could not keep women in order, could not enforce discipline and could not make them show proper fear and respect to their Master. The story of how he had used me to replace a dead girl might come out. No wonder he was furious!

"Silence, you dog of a Christian!" I heard him scream from behind me in Lingua Franca. "You not dare say one word in front of Master!"

Again the whip crashed down. I screamed again. I was doubled up in agony.

"Get back into position!" Hastily and abjectly I did so.

"Please forgive infidel dog, Effendi," said the angry Negro, bowing deeply. "She not yet properly broken in."

"Doubtless she has now learnt her lesson," came the dry reply from Hassan Ali, again in Lingua Franca. I was to learn that in Marsa it was widely used, especially by slave dealers and Negroes in charge of white women, for many men preferred to keep their slave girls ignorant of Arabic.

"Yes, indeed, Effendi."

"These women look fit and well," continued Hassan Ali, "I must congratulate you, Bashir Aga. We must press on now and decide how best to use them, for my guest, Hussein Bey, and I have other matters to discuss. But meanwhile, Your Excellency," he said turning towards the Bey, "you might be amused by seeing how we decide the fate of these Christian dogs."

Out of the corner of my eye I saw the Bey nod his agreement. No one seemed to have realised that my outburst was in English, nor that the Bey would have understood it. They were used to white women speaking outlandish languages - hence the importance attached to the use of Lingua Franca. But surely Rory, the Bey, would at any moment demand my release.

"Heads up!" came the well rehearsed order from the black eunuch. We all dutifully raised our heads, and straightened our arms whilst remaining on all fours. We looked straight ahead. With our breasts hanging down below us, and our buttocks thrust up, we must have made an erotic sight.

I did not dare to look sideways again towards the Bey. Anyway I was overcome with shame at being naked in front of him - and indeed in front of all the other beautifully dressed men.

As I knelt, on display, at the feet of these domineering and self confident men I could not help comparing them with many European men, hen-pecked by women and insecure in their presence. But there was nothing insecure or weak about these bastards! And yet in some curious way, being treated like this, although it outraged me, seemed to satisfy some primaeval feminine instinct. I could scarcely believe it, but I could feel my loins becoming thrillingly moist at being treated as a mere animal by these men, particularly in front of the Bey.

I knew that he would looking at my prettily hanging breasts, at my delicately shaped neck, at my slim waist and long back, at my flaring hips, at my little nose and at my soft little bottom, and comparing them with those of the other women. I blushed deeply - but when was he going to make a move about having me released?

Suddenly Bashir Aga called out in his high pitched voice: "Number 746!"

Carlotta, the buxom young Italian mother-to-be who had befriended me, dropped her head to the floor in a gesture of utter servility. The Negro eunuch unlocked the metal projection at the end of the bar, and slipped the ring of her collar off the bar, holding it in his hand. He touched her buttocks with his whip and led her up to the dais. She crawled along at his feet like an obedient dog, her lowered eyes wide open with fear. Out of the corner of my eye I saw her reach forward with her tongue. She began to lick our Master's shoes. The whip cracked. I shivered, How I hated and feared that whip! I saw her prettily kiss the hem of our Master's robe.

Soon it would be my turn.

"Up!" the Negro ordered.

Carlotta knelt up, her legs wide apart, her hands clasped behind her neck. The men all looked at her with interest. Her belly was just beginning to show her condition.

The eunuch was consulting his list, written in Arabic. He could read Arabic, I could not. He was my superior.

"Age 20. Italian. Well educated. Married and two months pregnant, for the first time, by her husband."

He paused, whilst several of the men on the dais made notes.

"Stand up!"

I did not dare look at her, but I knew that she would now be standing at attention, looking straight ahead.

47

"Jump!"

Poor Carlotta! I could hear her chains clinking as she jumped up and down to show herself off better to these odious men.

"Show Respect!"

I knew that they would be enjoying the sight of a helpless Christian girl having to display her shorn intimacies to them in such an abject way. Surely, I thought, the Bey must soon put a stop to all this. He was, after all, a civilised man. Then I remembered his phrase: "All my European girls fear me." I shuddered.

I could see that Carlotta was now turning, with her knees bent and her legs wide apart, in the humiliating way that we had had to practice, displaying herself to the men on the left and then on the right, whilst they discussed her amongst themselves. It must have been unbelievably degrading.

"Well? What shall we do with her?" asked Hassan Ali in his rather bored voice. "Sell her now as a pregnant slave, or keep her for the child?"

"Probably too tall to work satisfactorily at a loom," came a voice, presumably that of the carpet factory master.

"Probably not strong enough to make a good field slave," said another.

"Some of the brothels might be interested in her present condition," came another voice.

"... and with her good sized breasts she might become an excellent milk slave," came another voice that must have been the Master of Milk Slaves. "I should like to see her crawl again. Even if we don't keep her, we might sell her very well as a wet nurse." They watched poor Carlotta being led round and round on all fours.

"Right!" I heard Hassan Ali decide. "For milk."

He turned to the Bey. "I dare say your whipmaster would take her for a few months? A spell at the oars does wonders to firm up a woman's breasts."

I did not understand what he meant. Then I heard the familiar drawling voice of the Bey. "I'm sure we can find room for her!" I was still mystified as Carlotta was led out of the room.

"Number 384!" called out our hated overseer. She was a rather stolid looking girl of peasant stock, who was quickly put through her paces and allocated to the Field Slave Master.

"Next!" called out Hassan Ali impatiently.

The next woman was Inez, the older Spanish girl. She had always been trying to get into Bashir Aga's good books by reporting the rest of us, and often me, to him for minor misdemeanours. "She was the one who was talking!" she would say, pointing to me. "She's not trying," she would say maliciously, when in fact I was straining hard to raise the heavy above my head at the morning exercises. Several times I had got the whip because of her. I hated her, and her superior Spanish ways.

Suddenly I heard the supercilious sounding voice of the Bey.

"I believe I am allowed two of these women as my share for having provided a team of my Janissaries for the Corso," he said casually.

"Indeed, my dear friend, you can have any two you like." Clearly he and Hassan Ali were close business collaborators.

"Then I should like to have this one. My whipmaster tells me that he will soon be short of a couple of oars. I think he could make something of this one."

I glimpsed her give a sly smile to the Bey. I was furiously jealous. Obviously she had managed to catch his eye by smiling at him and giving the impression that she was obedient and passionate, rolling her big eyes at him. What a minx! I hated her more than ever. But what on earth did the Bey mean by his talk of 'being short of a couple of oars' and who was this whipmaster, whom he

49

had mentioned in connection with poor Carlotta? It would be several months before I learned the full horror of what he was so casually talking about.

"Of course you can have her, my friend. I will have her caged ready for you take with you. Don't forget you've still got to choose one more."

Suddenly my heart was pounding. One more to choose! This then was how he was planning to save me! He would ask for me as his final part of the booty! Obviously he and his page boy had recognised me when I called out before I was flogged into silence. Obviously he had claimed the other awful girl so as not to draw undue attention to me when he claimed me.

I could hardly wait for my turn to be inspected. But how shame-making that he, an Irishman, should have helped this terrible Corso. I had thought of him as a knight in shining armour coming to rescue a poor captive maiden, not as an active supporter of the whole dreadful system.

Still no matter, I was about to be rescued!

"Next!" called Hassan Ali.

"Effendi!" said Bashir Aga proudly, "This time, two together! Mother and daughter! Very special! Numbers 451 and 452!"

The Condessa and her daughter dropped their heads to the floor together. Then side by side they were led, crawling, up to the dais. Nervously they both licked the sole of his slipper, their tongues almost touching, and then kissed the hem of his robe.

"Ages thirty five and eighteen. Italian aristocrats. Plenty of money for ransom."

I saw Hassan Ali turn suddenly to his Breeding Manager.

"Stand up!" They stood at attention side by side, naked, looking more like sisters than mother and daughter. Clearly the Condessa had had the time and money to care for her body.

50

"Show respect!" I saw from behind a flush spread across their necks as they both assumed the degrading position and went through the awful routine.

"A well bred pair, eh?" came the voice of the Master. "I don't think we want to rush the ransoms. Let them each first make a contribution to your future blond breeding chain, Achmet. Or perhaps even two! We ought to make the most of a blonde mother and daughter ...! Oh," he turned to the Bey, "any chance of reserving a couple of places for this pair as well? It makes for a quick clean delivery and I don't want to risk any complications."

"I'm sure we can find room for them," replied the Bey with a laugh.

Once again I wondered what on earth they were talking about.

The poor Condessa had broken down into hysterical sobs and her daughter was crying, as they were both led away. But I was too excited about myself to waste much sympathy on them. In a few minutes I would be free!

Chapter 7

REJECTED!

"Number 632!"

I felt a tug on my collar. On all fours, like an animal, I was led up to the foot of the dais. I could feel the men's eyes assessing my naked body, judging my potential as a milk slave from the hang of my breasts, or from the muscles of my thighs my potential as a field slave or dancing girl in a brothel or harem. I was just an animal being judged. I was merely Slave Number 632, with the number tattooed on my forearm to prove it. But within minutes I would be free!

Suddenly I saw the soles of Hassan Ali's slippers in front of me. I could not lick them, not in front of the Bey! I simply could not do it.

"No, no!" I cried, "I won't do it. I won't."

I suppose such recalcitrance was almost unknown. This whole performance was intended to be a demonstration of a woman's obedience, not of her Irish temper!

Twice the whip fell across my back, the tip coming up and catching my breasts. I screamed. Beaten into submission, I began to lick.

I did not dare show my disgust. I did not dare even glance up at the Bey. I was too ashamed. Indeed I wondered if I would ever be able to look him in the face again, now that he had seen me do this.

The whip cracked. I crawled forward and took the hem of Hassan Ali's brocade robe in both hands and began to kiss it fervently. I remembered what our overseer had said about him. He was a rich and powerful man. He owned me, a mere slave. He could do what he liked with me. My very life was in his hands. I shivered with fright, momentarily forgetting that I was about to be freed and thinking only of the terrible whip.

"Up!"

I knelt up. Blushing, I parted my knees. I looked straight ahead, my head up, my shoulders back, my hands clasped behind my neck.

"Number 632! Age twenty two. Corsican. A virgin."

So the dead girl had been a couple of years younger than me. So I now came from Corsica! Miss Barbara Kennedy had completely disappeared, so far as Marsa was concerned. Enquiries would never find me now. Thank God the Bey knew who I really was.

Shyly I displayed myself. What would the Bey think of me now? I felt so ashamed, naked in front of him - and with my body hair removed.

But at least the Bey was a European man. And, anyway, I would never see him again once I had arrived safely back in Malta. Indeed all this would then simply seem like a bad dream.

"Stand up!" Hastily I jumped up, and stood at attention. I could not help eyeing the eunuch's whip anxiously.

"Jump!" Shamefacedly I started to jump and down. I could feel my breasts bouncing like mad.

"Show Respect!" I parted my legs and bent my knees in the way that I had been taught. But this time it was in front of real men. It really was a most degrading position. I could feel myself blushing all over. Keeping my feet wide apart and my knees bent I awkwardly turned my whole body in a shuffling movement towards the men on the left.

I glanced for a second at the Bey. His eyes were fixed on me. He was smiling. He was going to save me!

Still keeping my legs wide apart and my knees bent, I turned to the right. Time to turn round. I hesitated. I simply could not do it. Not in front of real men.

"No!" I cried. "Oh no!"

But the cunning Bashir Aga must have been expecting I might jib at this part of the ever more degrading routine. His whip came whistling down again across my back. With a sob I turned and pulled my buttocks apart, displaying myself most intimately, again to left and then to right.

"Allah has sent me a fiery one here!" I heard Hassan Ali say behind me. "She'll clearly need a lot of disciplining before being sold as a harem slave, but I think she would be rather wasted as a field slave ... What do you think, Bey? Would you like this creature as your second share of this booty?"

I heard him clear his throat. The waiting was awful.

Then he spoke slowly and clearly, as if wanting to be sure that I understood.

"No thank you! Certainly not! I don't want an arrogant bad tempered, unwilling bitch like her. She'd be a bad influence on my other girls. On no, the obstinacy would have to be thrashed out of her before I'd be interested in her! Maybe she'd make a good brothel slave if she's properly trained."

My mouth fell wide open in astonishment. I could not believe what I was hearing. Was he playing some deep game? He couldn't really mean what he had said. I was an Irish woman in distress! He must rescue me, he must!

"And I should put Bashir Aga in charge of her training. He won't stand any more of her nonsense after her performance today," I heard the Bey add.

Holy Mother of God, he was serious!

"Yes, I was thinking of putting him in charge of the next brothel training class," I heard Hassan Ali say.

"Would you like that, Bashir Aga? A chance to rectify this slave's attitude! Eh?"

"Assuredly, Master," I heard the awful black eunuch reply.

"That is settled then."

I was in a daze. I simply could not believe what I had heard. He was abandoning me! Worse, he made certain that I going to a fate worse than death - brothel training! I was to be trained as a prize whore! And by same awful whipmaster as we had had in the waggon.

I, a respectable Irish convent girl, a governess in the household of a British Ambassador, was to be sent for brothel training by a swine of an Arab slave dealer! And all because I was considered by that swine of a renegade Irish Bey to be too arrogant, too self-opinionated.

Then in a sudden flash, I realised that he was getting his revenge for the way that I had insulted him in Malta, and for slapping his face in public. Oh why could I not have kept my mouth shut, and my temper under control?

How I hated him! But in a strange way I wasn't sure that I really did.

Then through my sobs I vaguely heard the supercilious voice of the Bey again. Yes, I did hate him - or did I?

"May I take this opportunity to raise another matter, in which I should be grateful for your help?"

"Of course," replied Hassan Ali.

"As you know I've recently inherited my craft from my predecessor, together with his whipmaster. But I can only keep him for a few months. Do you think you could lend me Bashir Aga - when he's finished your brothel training class? He's just the sort of man I need to whip my sluts into shape!"

"How long would you want him for?"

"Oh, for about a year. But don't worry, I'd pay well for his services. I suggest I pay you ten times what ever you get for that miserable girl in the slave market after Bashir Aga has finished training her. That couldn't be fairer!"

"Would you be happy with that, Bashir Aga?" asked Hassan Ali.

"It would be an honour to serve His Excellency the Bey," came the suave reply of the black eunuch.

"Good, then that also is settled," laughed Hassan Ali.

Again I could scarcely believe my ears. He did not want me, pretty as I was, yet he would pay ten times my value for the awful Negro overseer's assistance in some vague enterprise concerning some craft - boat? - and the forcible use of white women.

And to think that this was the man whom I had relied upon to save me from the sheer horror of all this!

Chapter 8

PROCESSED

I found myself in the holding room next to the display room.

There was straw on the floor in case of accidents resulting from the women realising the full horror of the fate to which they had just been condemned. There were also several strong tethering posts and tethering rings cemented into the wall.

I was led past a small cage standing on a table. In it, gripping the bars, was Inez, the hated sneak, that the Bey had chosen as part of his share of the booty. I saw that she was smiling behind the bars. My feeling of jealousy flared up again. Why had he chosen her and not me? I wanted to scratch her eyes out!

The ring at the end of my collar chain was locked to one of the tethering rings. Across the room I saw the Condessa and her daughter, chained to the same ring. Carlotta and the peasant girl were chained to other rings. A young Negro, whip in hand, was enforcing strict silence.

I could hear the raised voices of the men next door as each woman was presented and judged. Sometimes, to my anguish, I heard the distinctive voice of the Bey. Every few minutes another of my companions was led into the room and secured to the appropriate tethering ring depending on the task to which she had been allocated: breeding, field work, harem training, milk, or brothel training.

To my rage I saw that a petite French girl, Dominique, was being put into the same small cage as Inez. She must have been the Bey's second choice! I felt overcome with chagrin at the thought that it might have been me. Instead he had chosen this chit of a girl. But why hadn't he chosen me instead? Because I had once been rude and disrespectful, and had slapped his face?

But I wouldn't do it again! I'd be obedient and submissive. I would, I promised, I would! But it was too late now. Thanks to my temper I was to be trained as a whore!

I heard the men next door going away. No doubt they were busy men and had to get back to their various enterprises. They had decided our fate, and were now leaving us to their Negro assistants. They themselves were Arabs. Arabs did not sully themselves handling animals, or Christian dogs like us! They left that to the Negro overseers. Indeed at that very moment several black overseers came into the room to take charge of their particular group of women.

Six of us had been chosen for Brothel Training, and three for Harem Training. The other three were, I had to admit, prettier, but we were more intelligent! Bashir Aga unlocked the rings of our collars. He was now in charge of our class, which I was to learn consisted of us six plus several other girls. He held the rings of our collar chains in one hand, like a kennelman holding the leads of a batch of dogs. As usual, there was a whip in his other hand.

He led us to another building. Beyond it was an open forge, several horses tethered around it. One was was being shoed by a burly Negro blacksmith. I did not think that he was a eunuch. He grinned and waved at Bashir Aga.

"The usual treatment?" he asked.

"The usual," replied our overseer. Then, pointing at me and two of the other girls, he added, "but these ones are virgins."

He tethered us by our collar chains, hanging the rings over a line of hooks out of our reach. We white women were smaller than these Negro giants and could not reach as high as them. We stood there naked and helpless, amongst the horses, waiting our turn.

I shivered with fear. The sight of white hot iron being beaten into shape, the heat from the forge, and the sheer brute strength of the Negro blacksmith, all this scared me stiff.

And I was also wondering anxiously just how we virgins were going to be treated differently from the other girls who had also been selected for brothel training, but who had been married before they were captured.

I longed to call out, and to ask with an ingratiating smile what was going to happen to us. But I did not dare do so. I had already been thrashed twice that day for speaking out of turn. In Marsa, I had learnt, white slave women only spoke, even to Negro slaves, when spoken to. I saw the blacksmith's shoulder muscles were huge. The strength in his right arm, his whipping arm, must have been very great. Near his forge hung a whip. The mere sight of it was enough!

After several horses had been shod, the blacksmith came over to me. I shrank back. Without a word, he reached up and lifted the ring of my chain off the hook and led me over to the forge. I could feel the heat on my naked body. He fastened the ring to another hook and made me kneel down by his anvil. I was terrified.

He picked up a riming instrument and a hammer and pushed my neck down onto the anvil. A quick blow of his hammer knocked the lead pellet out of the flanges on the side of my iron collar. He opened the collar and took it off me. Then he reached up and took down a new shiny brass collar that was much wider than the previous one. It had a large ring on the front and another at the back.

It was strangely beautiful. He checked that it fitted tightly round my neck and under my chin, which was now kept pushed up. He seemed satisfied. He inserted a lead pellet into the closure, and with another instrument he squeezed it shut. The new brass collar had now been riveted round my neck.

Then the Negro blacksmith picked up a shiny brass disc with some Arabic writing on it. He threaded a strong looking ring through a small hole in the disc, then passed this ring through the ring on the front of my collar, and used a large instrument to force it shut. My collar now carried the name of my owner. If I changed owner, then, I suppose, a new disc would be attached to my collar. The disc tinkled against my collar with my every movement, reminding me of my slave status.

Then he turned and reached for a length of light chain some two feet in length. On either end were manacles. He put one manacle over over each wrist, inserted the lead pellets and squeezed them shut - I was now permanently manacled.

He measured my waist and wrote down a figure. Then he kicked aside my legs and, very embarrassingly, measured the distance from my naval down between my legs to my rear orifice, and wrote that down too. Holding the measurements in his hand, he went over to a rack on which were hanging a line of strange looking brass belts. Choosing one that apparently corresponded with the measurements, he came back and put it round my waist. It fastened behind me in the small of my back.

But hinged onto the front of the belt was a U-shaped piece of brass that went down between my legs. The Negro blacksmith pulled it up tight from behind. In the front was a heart shaped piece that had been specially shaped, curved and flattened to fit neatly over a girl's intimacies. There was Arabic writing engraved on this piece - the name of my Master again.

Low down on the heart shaped piece, just below my beauty bud, was a narrow slit. Because the belt was drawn up tight between my legs, my now hairless beauty lips, tightly compressed, were forced out between the sides of the slit. My beauty lips were thus well displayed, and liquids could be passed, but nothing, not even a little finger, could be put up inside me.

Level with the bottom of my beauty lips, the bottom of the heart shaped piece was attached to a shaped small brass rod that went up tightly between my buttocks to the belt in the small of my back, where the Negro fastened it with a padlock. The rod would not impede the passing of wastes.

I had been fastened into a very effective form of chastity belt. The Arabs of North Africa were of course well known for their skill in brass work.

The Negro now patted my naked bottom and made me stand in the yard, whilst he repeated the operation on the next girl. Only us virgins were fitted with a chastity belt. Evidently our virginity was a valuable asset that our owner was determined to protect so as to get a price for us when our training was complete.

Horrified by all this, I thought of running away. But where could I go, naked, with my wrists chained and with a collar riveted round my neck bearing my Master's name? How would I get over the high wall surrounding the estate?

When he had finished with the next girl, he made me stand behind her. He snapped a six foot length of light chain onto the ring on the front of my new collar, and snapped the other end onto the ring at the back of the other girl's collar, then repeated the process with each girl in turn.

By now Bashir Aga had returned. He thanked the blacksmith, and took the key to our chastity belts. Then he snapped a lead onto the ring on the front of the leading girl's collar. He gave it a tug. We followed him. We had been coffled.

He led us down a path to another building with bars on the windows. From inside I heard the sound of Arabic music, and what seemed to be the hesitant voice of a European girl trying to sing in the wailing Moorish way. I heard the tinkling of little bells in time with the music. A whip cracked. A girl cried out.

"I'll try harder, Sir! I promise! Please don't beat me any more!"

Our overseer, now our trainer, motioned us to stand still. He knocked on the door of the building.

My breaking in and training as a brothel slave, as a whore, was about to begin!

PART TWO

TRAINED TO BE A WHORE

Chapter 9

THE FEEDING TROUGH

"When I say eat, Christian pig, you eat!"

The warning came from behind me as I knelt in front of the long wooden trough, hands flat on the floor.

The speaker was black, strong and cunning. He was ugly and repulsive with small pig-like eyes, and tribal scaring decorating his face. He was naturally cruel - a skilled and experienced overseer of white women slaves. He might be a slave, but he was worth twenty times more than me, pretty as I was. He was the Bashir Aga, the Beater of Women, and I hated him.

With his foot he pushed my face down into the sticky wet swill. I gasped for breath as the slimy porridge covered my face. At last I felt his foot lifted off my head. I raised my head slightly, the gruel dripping off my chin, my nose and my eye-brows. My mouth was full of the stuff. Quickly I swallowed the tasteless mixture of boiled oats, boiled barley and water, and thrust my face back into the trough before the eunuch's foot did it for me. Desperately I guzzled, I slurped, I sucked and I swallowed. I made as much noise as possible, resembling a pig at the trough, to show my whipmaster that I was eating it all up.

On either side of me the rest of the class were doing the same. The watery porridge was revolting, but it was cheap and nourishing. There were, I suppose, a couple of hundred white women slaves working on Hassan Ali's estate, or being trained or made ready for the market, and this swill was all that they got - except for a handful of dates which once a day was thrown into the porridge, together with the remains of Bashir Aga's own delicious meals.

If one of us performed very well during training, then that ghastly Bashir Aga might reward her by throwing a a piece of Turkish Delight, or some other sweetmeat, into the trough in front her. It was wonderful to taste something sweet again after nothing but that tasteless gruel. I hated being brought down to the level of a performing animal, but I just could not help longing to be rewarded with a sweet. I was so jealous when one was awarded to another girl.

Twice I had been awarded a sweet. On the first occasion the girl kneeling next to me, a French girl, had, greatly daring, put her head into the trough ahead of me and, quick as a flash, had snatched the precious piece of Turkish Delight with her teeth. Neither of us had dared to raise our hands off the floor and so, like dogs fighting over a bone, we had fought with our teeth over that piece of Turkish Delight. Finally I had managed to get a little bit of it back.

As usual we had been fed naked. Officially, this may have been so that we did not dirty our tunics, but Bashir Aga clearly used it as a way of driving home our animal-like servility, which was why he made us eat like animals out of a trough. That's why the cruel brute also kept us naked when we were locked up in our cages.

But for the rest of the time we were allowed to wear our scandalously short and really rather provocatively cut silken tunics. No matter how scandalous these skimpy tunics might have been regarded in Europe, we all were delighted to be allowed to wear something. I loved my little tunic, though I hated the Arabic writing on the right breast that proclaimed, once again, that I was the property of Hassan Ali. And I hated the huge Arabic numbers, my slave number 632, that I had been made to embroider right across the back of the tunic.

The tunics were blue and white, the colours of the House of Hassan Ali. I could not help blushing every morning when we had to step up one at a time in front of the seated young black boy, who was Bashir Aga's assistant, and lift up the front of our tunics so that he could part and inspect our beauty lips. The loathsome boy would then call out the result for Bashir Aga to record in his book, before rubbing the burning depilatory cream across our mounds and down along the lips.

It was all very humiliating and the fact that it was done by a mere boy made it even worse.

Sometimes my Irish temper made me want to knock his hand aside, to scream that I was a British girl, that they had no right to treat me in such a degrading way. But the sight of his cane would quickly bring me to my senses.

The knowledge that all the other white women in Hassan Ali's various enterprises would also be undergoing a similar daily inspection and removal of body hair by their black overseers scarcely made it any better.

In my case the boy would also unlock my brass chastity belt so that he could get a better feel, the young swine. I would have to stand in front of him, looking straight ahead, my legs apart and my knees bent, holding up not only my tunic but also the U-shaped piece of the belt. I would bite my lips to keep silent, as he first probed and examined and then as I felt the stinging cream doing its work. Then he would order me to turn sideways so that he could pull the belt up tightly behind and lock it again, whilst making sure that my lips, pinched by the slit, were well displayed - like the petals of flower.

Surprisingly enough the belt, with its curved brass edges, was quite comfortable to wear, but every morning, and indeed frequently throughout the day, I would curse that swine of a Protestant ascendancy Irishman, that so-called Bey, who to get his revenge had condemned me to this dreadful degradation.

These tunics, and the longer silken caftans that we were sometimes allowed to wear, played an important part in our frequent deportment lessons when we had to practice the art of arousing a man by the way that we walked, swinging the skirts, as well as our buttocks and breasts. We also had to learn the art of rubbing the silk material against a potential client's skin and then erotically slipping out of the silk.

Both the tunics and the caftans were fastened with a button on each shoulder so that, despite our permanently manacled wrists, we could easily put them on or take them them off. Except for the chastity belts worn by us virgins, we were never allowed to wear anything else.

A week or so after our training began I stupidly allowed myself to become involved in an attempted revolt against the humiliating way in which we were being treated and the awful things we were being made to learn. The ring leader was a woman who kept saying that if we were going to a fate worse than death, then we should risk death. She persuaded several of us to go on a hunger strike to force them to move us to more respectable work.

So when the first gong went as a signal for us to lower our heads into the trough, we just knelt there with our heads up smiling at each other. I had feared a terrible explosion from Bashir Aga and the sight of the cane in his hand quickly made me regret ever having agreed to take part in the hunger strike.

However, he had clearly been expecting some such revolt. Quickly grabbing our leader, he bundled her into a tiny cage which we had seen lying empty in the corner of the feeding room. It was so small that she could hardly move. She had to lie curled up with her neck chained just below some sliding bars.

The rest of us were taken one at a time and put into a sort of stocks, with our neck and wrists held in a pillory. I was first. Bashir Aga had decided to make an example of me - knowing my Irish temper. He put a special gag into my mouth, which made me keep my mouth wide open and stopped me from biting. It was strapped behind my neck and had a circular hole in the centre, through which he pushed a tube down into my stomach. I shook my head wildly in protest, but there was nothing I could do. With a plunger, he then forced food down into my stomach. It was horrible. I could not even taste the food. It was just forced straight into my stomach.

Then my gag was removed. The powerful black eunuch pointed silently at the trough. My will-power was now completely broken. With a sob of despair I nodded obediently. He unfastened me from the stocks and clapped his hands. Like a well trained performing animal I crawled to the trough and lowered my head. Slowly and ponderously he came over to me and with his foot pushed my head into the slave gruel ...

He repeated the process with each of the other three girls who had tried to go on hunger strike.

From then on, just to remind us of our foolishness in challenging his authority, he would periodically thrust one of our faces deep into the trough, just as he had done to me earlier that day with his foot. We never knew when, or to which of us, he was going to do it to. He certainly put the fear of God into us. Never again was there the slightest sign of any revolt, not even when he made us do the most disgusting things.

The girl who had led the hunger strike suffered a much harsher fate. She was kept in her tiny cage for weeks and forcibly fed with the tube half a dozen times a day, and not with our innocuous slave gruel but only with milk and cream. Soon she became enormous. When she was finally allowed out of her cage, she was so fat she she could hardly stand. There was, it seemed, quite a demand in Moorish brothels for such women. It was a terrible lesson for the rest of us.

From the very start of our dreadfully humiliating training we had been terrorised. Of course the House of Hassan Ali had had years of experience of first breaking in respectable and horrified white women, and then training them to be whores in the high class brothels of Marsa. We were only the latest of many similar classes, and the techniques used to reduce us to a state of complete obedience, like well schooled horses, must have been developed over many years.

As part of this breaking-in, our entire class of a dozen young women had at first been incarcerated at night in a dark underground dungeon. We had to hang up our tunics outside and go into it naked. The floor was quite bare. We had no blankets, beds or carpets. In the darkness rats began to appear. We were terrified. Girls were screaming as they felt rats scrambling over them in the dark.

Then Bashir Aga told us that, if we cooperated fully and if he received good reports on us from all our instructors, then we would be moved out of the dungeon. Otherwise we would stay down there at night. Needless to say we all tried desperately hard to please our instructors and to overcome our disgust - all except one girl who remained sulky and resentful at being trained as a whore.

That evening when he locked us up again in the dreadful dungeon for the night, Bashir Aga pointed to her and said that until she mended her ways we would all stay in the dungeon at night. Hardly had the door shut when, led by me, the girls all flung themselves on her, biting and scratching her, pummelling her and pulling her hair. Screaming for mercy, she soon agreed that she really did want to learn to be a whore. In fact she later she became the most licentious of us all.

The following evening we were moved to a light and airy cage with straw on the floor and a bucket for our wastes. Then later we were each given our own cage, with a small piece of carpeting and half a blanket. But always hanging over us was the threat of being moved back into the terrifying dungeon.

The cages were too low to stand up in and too small to stretch out in, but each of us did have a tiny mirror and a simple hairbrush and comb, a small bowl of water and - the ultimate luxury - a small piece of soap.

They were in two rows, one above the other. The front of each was barred, so we had no privacy from the suspicious eyes of our overseer - or of his boy assistant. At night time a lantern burned continuously outside. You never knew when the hideous face of Bashir Aga would look into your cage, checking that you were not misbehaving.

But it was each girl's little home of her own, and each of us was allowed to decorate her place with a few pathetic flowers, picked in our exercise yard, or with a little piece of ribbon given to us as a reward by our dancing instructress. But every morning we had to leave our cages immaculate with the rug rolled up, and the carefully polished brass bowls for our wastes, together with the hairbrush and comb, positioned exactly in the regulation place. My true Irish feeling of independence made me want to revolt against such discipline, but I did not dare to do so.

I saw the terrifying Negro coming back up the line of feeding women. How I longed to spit in his face! But one glance at the cane he was carrying and I very quickly changed my ideas. Hastily I put my face back into the sticky porridge and started to guzzle it up again.

On the journey down to Marsa, Bashir Aga had carried a thick short whip with a stiff handle. Elsewhere on Hassan Ali's estate the black overseers carried short black whips which they cracked menacingly behind the white women in their charge. But here in the brothel training wing, Bashir Aga and his awful boy assistant carried long thin bamboo canes with a curved handle.

The constant threat of a caning dominated all our thoughts. It was quite terrifying. As I had learnt in the waggon, the whip was mainly used across a girl's back. Here, however, we had to hold out our hands for the cane like naughty school children, or bend over and lift up our tunics to bare our bottoms for it. Worst of all, the punishment for what the Negroes considered to be dumb insolence, or for answering back, was having to stand in front of the whole class to receive a 'Three times Three'.

The first time I saw a girl getting a 'Three times Three' by our overseer I just could not believe that anything so brutal could be done to a delicate young Christian woman - in this case to my friend Isabella.

It was shortly after we had started our training. Isabella was a young married woman of my own age from Sicily. We looked quite alike. She had just been married when corsairs raided the village where she and her rich husband had a villa. They had killed her husband and carried her off. She was an educated woman, a little taller and slimmer than me, with small pointed breasts unlike my more rounded ones. She had dark hair and brown friendly eyes and was always laughing.

She had been sentenced to a 'Three times Three' by our cruel Negro overseer for 'slackness', although he knew very well why she was feeling off colour that day. At the morning inspection, the nasty little Negro boy had humiliatingly called out when he had spotted the the first signs of the climax to her monthly cycle. But Bashir Aga was a real swine. He was determined to show us all that this was no excuse for not practising hard at our lessons.

That evening we had to kneel in a line on all fours. Poor Isabella had to stand facing us, her hands clasped behind her neck. She looked very frightened.

The black eunuch intoned, "In the name of Allah, the most Merciful." Then he swished his long whippy cane through the air several times. I could see the muscles of his naked torso rippling. He looked so huge, and Isabella looked so slight and helpless, that my heart went out to her. I wanted to hurl myself at the huge Negro, to scratch his eyes out, to snap his cane in two, to ... but I was too terrified even to move a finger. I just watched spellbound.

The Negro brought the cane down across the front of Isabella's thighs - a particularly sensitive place for a woman. She screamed and doubled up with pain.

The Negro raised the cane again. Again he intoned, "In the name of Allah the most Merciful."

Then unbelievably he brought the cane down across Isabella's soft little belly. Again she screamed and doubled up, clasping her stomach with the pain. Again he waited and then motioned her with his cane to stand up straight again, her head well up and her shoulders back. Again he intoned: "In the name of Allah the most Merciful."

This time, even more unbelievably, he brought the cane downright across her out-thrust breasts. Isabella screamed. She was sobbing and holding her burning little breasts.

"Now you listen carefully, you Christian pig," the Negro said in his high pitched voice, "for next three strokes, you stay quite still. You not move, you not cry out until after all three strokes. Then you cry and jump about until time for next three. You cry or move before and all three not count. Now kiss cane!"

71

I was horrified. No man had the right to treat an educated woman like that, and certainly not a brute of a Negro. A grown woman being thrashed by a black eunuch! And it might so easily have been me. Never, I told myself, will I ever be caught slacking, never will I ever be disrespectful.

Sobbing, Isabella kissed the cane. Oh how I hated that cane! It looked so slight and innocuous, but it ruled our lives.

The Negro had not yet finished degrading Isabella. "You now say, 'I am lazy slut and deserve to be punished. In the name of Allah, please cane me again.'" Sobbing, Isabella tried to say the words.

"No!" shouted the Negro. "You say it properly and clearly. All class want to hear!"

Shamefacedly Isabella called out the words again. She resumed her position, her hands raised behind her neck, her belly thrust forward. She was biting her lips. The Negro intoned his hateful tone and began again. Somehow Isabella managed to stifle her screams and hold her position. As the third stroke fell, leaving a red weal right across both breasts, she fell to her knees, clutching her them and then rubbing her belly and trying to stroke her thighs, as she sobbed her heart out.

Then once again she had to kiss the cane. Again she had to beg to be thrashed. Again she had to receive the three strokes on the front of her body.

It had been a truly terrifying lesson for the rest of us. It was a very subdued class that trotted in a line over to the corner of the room to have a Moorish singing lesson. All of us were determined to sing our our hearts out in the hideous Moorish way, rather than risk a 'Three times Three.'

The gong sounded twice.

Immediately we all lifted our faces from the trough and knelt up. One stroke of the gong was the signal to start eating, two to stop - to stop at once. There was still a lot of the revolting looking porridge in the trough. It would remain there, congealing, until our evening meal, when it must all be eaten up and the trough licked spotlessly clean.

The gong was struck three times.

We all knelt forward and scraped the porridge off our faces on the side of the trough. None must be wasted, but we were not allowed to use our hands. Not until later would we be allowed to wash it off.

I glanced down the line at the other virgins in the class with their highly polished brass chastity belts locked round their loins. We virgins had to spend hours polishing our wretched chastity belts. Oh how I hated mine, and yet I could not help also being rather proud of the way my virginity was being safeguarded. But kept for whom, I also could not help wondering? I had always planned to return home to Ireland to marry Dermot as soon as he had inherited his farm, and I had been jealously keeping my virginity for him. Now would it be taken from me by force? Would I ever see my Dermot again?

It was not easy, with my chained wrists, to polish the belt, particularly behind. But I soon learned that if Bashir Aga saw the slightest speck of dirt on it, then you got the cane. Once he had found a little piece of dirt on the thin bar that went up up between the cheeks of my buttocks, or so he said, and I had been given six strokes across the palms of my hands. It had hurt like all the demons of hell itself, and from then on I had always asked Isabella to check every morning that my belt was gleamingly spotless - everywhere.

The horribly cunning thing about the belt was that the slit through which my body lips were forced, and through which it was quite impossible to get even a little finger, only started just below my beauty bud. Try as I might, when I thought that Bashir Aga or his wretched Negro boy assistants were not watching, I could not reach my precious little bud with my finger. And I soon found that touching my lips alone was a poor substitute - as Bashir Aga well knew, for he scarcely bothered to check, as he did constantly with the other girls, that we virgins were not misbehaving, alone or with each other.

The belt was never removed for passing water, even though of course this had to be done under supervision, nor was it removed when passing wastes. Indeed I soon learned that the thin, tight, and highly polished, metal bar was no real impediment to that. It did, however, ensure my second virginity - though I was shocked and horrified to learn that the awful Moors enjoyed using both women and boys in such a way. Certainly the very idea had never even been whispered about in my convent school in Ireland.

Holy Mother of Christ, it was all just too awful. What sort of men were these Moors? They were crueler than anything I had ever imagined could exist on this earth. There was just no limit to their casual cruel attitude towards their white Christian slave women.

Except for us virgins, locked into our chastity belts, the rest of the class had to sleep with a brass phallus inserted every evening in the particular orifice that in our case was protected by our thin tight bar. Horrified we learned that this was to make it easier for a Moor to penetrate them there. During the night, Bashir Aga or the boy would thrust their hands through the bars of the other women's cages to check that the shiny brass instrument was still in place. Woebetide any girl who was found to have slipped hers out!

We virgins were excused this degrading preparation. A brothel owner buying us must be able to check our total virginity as much by our tightness there, as by the continuing existence of our protecting hymen in another orifice.

It was a few days after our hated overseer had put the leader of our attempted revolt into the tiny fattening cage that he sprang his next surprise.

He said that up to now we had just been a disorganized rabble, but that now he was going to appoint a Head Girl for our class. She would be responsible to him for the discipline of the class at all times. She would not carry a whip, but she could report any girl who misbehaved to him for punishment. Her symbol of authority would be her pencil and notebook, in which she was to keep a record of all our misdemeanours. Most important of all, she herself would not get the cane whilst she remained Head Girl.

We all discussed who was going to be chosen. Bashir Aga was watching us all closely and each of us was on our best behaviour, hoping to be chosen - and not the get cane any more.

I naturally assumed that I would be made the Head Girl. Although I had been cowed by Bashir Aga's cane, I was still the most outspoken girl in the class - and the most intelligent. And I had been Head Girl at my convent school - so I knew the ropes.

I was horrified therefore when the Negro announced that the French girl Louise, or Number 753 to give her her proper slave name, had been chosen. She was the wife of a young French army officer. She had been captured when she was on her way to join her husband in Naples. She was a big girl and very strong. I hated her. We all did. She was the girl who had seized my hard earned piece of Turkish Delight in the feeding trough. She had done the same to other girls. None of us could beat her in a fight. That's why the cunning Negro had chosen her to be Head Girl and not me.

Bashir Aga had already imposed strict military discipline and drill. We had learned to line up between lessons in strict order of height, tallest on the right and shortest on the left. We had learned always to move at the double, keeping in step and always raising our knees high in the air in an exaggerated and provocative way. Now Louise would be our lead girl. When we lined up, she was on the right, two paces clear of the right hand girl, to show her superior position. When we were ordered to turn smartly to the right and double off, she was in front and set the pace. We had to keep in step with her.

From now on, whenever a girl had earned a sweet, it was given to Louise to give to the girl. She would always take a big bite out of it first. She also stood by Bashir Aga and his boy assistant at the humiliating morning inspections of our intimacies, smiling at our embarrassment. She was responsible for inspecting the spotless cleanliness of our chastity belts. We hated her more than ever, but we also feared her. She now had power, the power of our overseer's cane.

At first when she reported us for any misconduct, or insolence to her, it was an automatic two strokes of the cane. Then after a week, the Negro told us, as we lined up in front him, looking straight ahead, with shoulders back and bellies sucked in, that he was pleased with the hated Louise as Head Girl. In future any girl reported by her for punishment would get four strokes.

She smiled with pleasure. Oh how I longed to pull the bitch's beautiful hair, to scratch her eyes out and to push her face into the filthy porridge!

Chapter 10

BROTHEL TRAINING AND THE BEY

"Show respect!" ordered our black overseer as several young Negroes came into the room and lined up. Hastily we all parted our legs. It was, of course, a punishable offence to keep your legs together in the presence of a man.

The class was also lined up, as usual kneeling on all fours, along one side of the room, facing the Negroes. Bashir Aga nodded and they removed their loincloths. It was almost the first time that I had seen a naked man close up, and certainly the first time I had seen a naked Negro. I was astonished by the size of their manhoods, and shocked and repelled. I looked down in disgust and embarrassment.

"Pay attention, 632! Look up!" shouted Bashir Aga

Quickly I raised my head. I did want to risk a 'Three Times Three'.

An attractive white woman of about thirty came into the room. She was dressed like us in a slave tunic, but with a red sash. She was a Junior Instructress. But she still wore a brass slave collar like us, and her hands were still manacled by a length of chain.

She knelt at the feet of the first Negro. Bashir Aga snapped his fingers. She licked his feet. As she did so I saw marks of the cane across her now exposed bottom. So even a a woman so high above us was still subjects to slave discipline! I felt sorry for her. Our black overseer again snapped his fingers. She knelt up and bared her breasts, then licked the Negro's muscular thighs, slowly and adoringly.

Again came the snap of Bashir Aga's fingers. She raised her manacled hands.

"Look carefully, you little sluts," ordered Bashir Aga. "See how she uses just the tips of her fingers and the sight of her breasts to excite the man."

Horrified, and yet somehow fascinated, I watched as the Negro's manhood slowly sprang into erection. It was huge. I could not take my eyes off it. It made me feel small and utterly subservient.

I was even more shocked when Bashir Aga again snapped his fingers, for the woman now lowered her head and took the huge black manhood into her mouth. There was a sucking noise.

The woman started to lick up and down the Negro's manhood.

"632!" he suddenly ordered. "You show class how well you have learned lesson. He pointed to another naked Negro standing alongside the one being pleasured by the woman.

"No! No!" I cried. "I couldn't!"

Bashir Aga's pig like little eyes glistened. He smiled as if anticipating such reluctance. Slowly he raised his cane, and with his other hand raised three fingers.

"Alright! Alright!" I screamed. Hastily I crawled forward on all fours to the Negro's feet. Bashir Aga snapped his fingers. Obediently, just as the woman had done, I lowered my head and began to lick them. They tasted horrible. They smelt horrible. It was my first taste encounter with the musky smell of a real Negro man.

But I did not dare stop, for Bashir Aga was now standing over me, his cane raised.

"You forget something," he said harshly. He gave my buttocks a hard tap. My God, my knees were tight together! Hastily I parted them - wide. A girl must still Show Respect even when arousing a man.

He snapped his fingers and the woman kneeling at my side gestured to her breasts. Shamefacedly I knelt up and pulled down my tunic. She again began to lick up her Negro's thighs. I copied her on mine.

I again heard the snap of fingers. I felt like a performing dog being taught a new trick. Nervously and hesitantly, I reached forward and touched the Negro's sack. I jumped back as I felt its shrivelled skin, but Bashir Aga's cane was ready and waiting for such a display of repulsion. He brought it down hard across my back. I screamed, but I started to use my fingers again.

The horrible musty smell became very strong, and it was with horror that I watched as the manhood slowly sprang into life under my eyes. I felt sick and yet somehow fascinated. I was indeed becoming a whore.

Again Bashir Aga snapped his fingers. I felt his iron hand grip my neck.

"Take it," he ordered.

I lowered my head with a sob. He was still gripping my neck. Terrified and appalled I opened my mouth and very gingerly touched the dark mauve coloured tip.

"Deep! Deep down!" came the order, accompanied by a sharp tap of the cane on my buttocks and a sudden tightening of the grip on my neck.

I was almost sick when I felt the huge tip touch the back of my throat, but the grip on my neck was remorseless. Then slowly I was allowed to come back for a few seconds.

"Copy me!" whispered the woman kneeling alongside me.

Soon I was copying the woman in taking the huge manhood in and out of my mouth, my head rising and falling. It was awful, but I did not dare stop. All I could think of was how I could never now look my betrothed, Dermot, in the face again. Perhaps it was just as well that it seemed unlikely, anyway, that I should ever see him again.

Suddenly out of the corner of my eye I saw someone enter the little gallery that looked down into the training room. I recognised the gross figure of our Master, Hassan Ali. In the background I vaguely saw a taller man accompanying him. I felt unbelievably degraded in being seen sucking a black manhood by them.

I heard the voice of Hassan Ali, speaking in Lingua Franca. "I thought, my friend, that you would like to see how this class is coming on."

"Well now, I never expected that that particular girl would be so keen on doing what she is now doing so avidly."

It was the distinctive arrogant voice of the Bey. He was looking at me doing this awful thing. I choked. I gasped. I almost stopped, but the cane whipped down across my buttocks again.

As my head went to and fro, I raised my eyes to the gallery. The Bey was looking at me intently. Never have I felt so degraded as at that moment.

"Come along, my friend," laughed Hassan Ali, leading the way out of the door that led into the gallery. The Bey followed him, leaving me shocked. But only for a moment.

"Get on 632!" ordered Bashir Aga. Again the cane came down, this time right across my back. Then after a few minutes, he called out, "Right 632, get back into line! Next girl!"

Thankfully I crawled to the line of waiting women.

Chapter 11

ADVANCED TRAINING

Bashir Aga was the instructor for many of our lessons but was joined for others by a variety of Negroes - all thoroughly enjoying degrading white women. The fact that they were black and male made it all the more humiliating and embarrassing.

Except for a short afternoon rest, the lessons seemed to go on all day in a bewildering succession. I seemed to be having dreadful lessons in everything that a woman could possibly be made to do, with the emphasis always being as girlish and pleasing as possible.

It was rather like being back at school, though the lessons were rather more advanced than at any girl's school I'd ever attended! And being disciplined by a huge Negro with a whip was rather different from the mild reproaches of the nuns.

They also made us practice endlessly running, both naked and wearing our pretty tunics, with our hands held out straight away from our sides, our hands bent back parallel to the floor, our fingers outstretched, our shoulders back and our breasts swinging excitingly. It was the childish way of moving that the Moors liked to see imposed on European women slaves.

We were also taught some simple Arabic expressions. We had to lisp and speak like little girls. It amused Moorish men to hear a grown up European woman being made to speak like a child. We were not allowed to address a Master as 'you', nor to use the word 'I'. We had to learn ridiculous expressions like:

"Can this little slave have her her kind Master's permission to speak?"

"Does this little slave please her big strong Master?"

"This little slave loves her Master."

"Would Master like his little slave to please him with her tongue?"

"Does Master want his little slave to fetch him a bowl?"

I was really shocked to learn that it was part of the duties of a slave girl, particularly a Christian one, to hold a bowl, sometimes with her teeth so as to keep her hands free, whilst a Master relieved himself, and to have to learn the complex cleaning and purifying rituals which we would also have to carry out for our Masters. At first I felt sick with disgust when we were made to practice this with huge Negro men whilst Bashir Aga stood over us, his cane in his hand, to make sure we did it properly and lovingly.

They made a point of not teaching us to read or write Arabic, nor did they allow us any European books or even writing materials. Later I was to learn that Moors liked to keep even their Moorish women illiterate. We did learn Arabic numerals, for they were tattooed onto our forearms, but nothing more.

Those swine forbade us to practice our Christian religion, and told us that since we only had the status of animals, it was 'unseemly' for us to be taught the Moslem religion. Nevertheless we had to learn about the importance to our Masters of the daily prayers, five times a day; about the subservient position of women; about how women must be strictly supervised; and about Friday prayers after which not only did public executions take place but also major punishment for women in harems and brothels.

I'd never bent my knee to any man, but now I had to learn to serve food and drink to a man on my knees, and in such a way that he would feel I was also offering my body for his use. It was horrible, but I had to do it, just as I had to practice parading up and down in front of a man choosing a woman for his pleasure; or undressing before a man in a slow and sensuous way; or bathing a man; or sitting up and begging for a scrap of delicious real food from a man's fingers; or belly dancing and singing; or, most important of all, assuming at a word of command the various positions and techniques used in the Moorish world to give a man pleasure.

The most humiliating lessons were those in which, under Bashir Aga's instruction, we had to practice entertaining a client by playing with ourselves or with each other. To have to do these intensely private things under the critical gaze of a Negro eunuch, and to his explicit orders, was quite unbelievably awful.

As I have said, I had never really seen any naked man close up before, never mind an aroused black one. I was appalled. However, Bashir Aga did not hesitate to use his cane at the first sign of hesitation in touching, licking, kissing and stroking the manhoods of these huge and terrifying men, or in assuming the most shameful positions with them.

Bashir Aga usually kept our chastity belts locked onto us virgins, but we would still have to watch whilst a Negro would thrust his huge manhood in turn into the bodies of the other girls, and then make them practice belly dance movements with their muscles to give him an exciting squeezing feeling - and woebetide any girl who failed to please the Negro who had penetrated her.

We were made to practice only with Negroes, because they knew that we were so repelled by them that we would not start enjoying ourselves. Nevertheless the girls being penetrated had to be careful lest, against their will, their bodies began to respond to the repeated thrusts of the Negro and to their own wriggling movements.

Bashir Aga had made it quite clear that whilst a client in a Moorish brothel might enjoy arousing us, and in keeping us aroused, nevertheless we would be thrashed if we ever climaxed without his express permission - and this applied to these lessons. We were terrified - and deeply humiliated by being warned about such a private matter by a man.

As for playing with ourselves, or with each other, although a client might well tell us to to do it in front of him for his amusement, if we did by ourselves in secret then that would be regarded as unfaithfulness - the punishment for which could perhaps be circumcision.

We were told horrific stories about this. The removal of the lips as well as the beauty bud itself was not common amongst Moorish women, but was widespread in black Africa. It was normally, but not always, done before puberty and resulted in just a long scar where normally there was a woman's beauty lips. A little tight orifice was left at the bottom to enable a man still to enjoy her. Some brothel owners found it paid to have some of their Christian girls done, as freaks, so as to bring in the clients. I was terrified by this barbaric way of treating white women.

A milder version was just to have a girl's beauty bud snipped off. This made it virtually impossible for her to reach a climax.

We were told that many brothel owners, like the rich owners of large harems, liked to have at least some of their white girls 'cut'. Quite apart from the mental satisfaction of keeping the girl frustrated, many Moors apparently swore that, since it prevented the girl from actually reaching a climax, it made the pleasure for themselves all the more prolonged and enjoyable.

Many Moslems, we were taught, took the view that a woman's beauty bud was an unnatural male vestige, rather like nipples on a man. Moreover, it enabled her to enjoy sex as much as a man, thus giving her ideas above her station, which was simply to give men pleasure and to mother the next generation of free men and slaves. It also, they said, made a woman promiscuous, constantly seeking pleasure from her own hands, from other women or from men other than her Master.

The Koran says that women were put into the world to give pleasure to men, not to receive pleasure themselves. Thus, many men would say that removal of a woman's beauty bud was only right and proper.

We were therefore very lucky, we were told, that Hassan Ali did not circumcise all his slaves, preferring to leave it to their eventual new Masters to decide whether to have them 'cut'.

I wondered if any of the girls in the Bey's harem had been circumcised. He was such an arrogant swine that I would not have been surprised if they had. I also could not help wondering what Dermot would think, if I ever got back to civilisation having been 'cut'.

I was also horrified to learn that Moorish men liked to have several slave girls in their beds at a time. The very idea! But even we virgins, locked into our chastity belts, were made to practice working with our tongues, mouths and finger tips, as one of a pair of girls, or even as one of a team of three or more.

Bashir Aga would stand over us cane in hand, directing us and pointing out to the shocked class the most stimulating caresses and the most sensitive places on a male body - as we saw from the varying state of arousal of the Negro stallion with whom we were practising. We had to learn to hold and play with his manhood, using both hands to arouse and keep him aroused, then finally to use our mouths to bring him to an exploding climax.

I'd always regarded myself as just as good as any man, and better than most. Now I had to learn that women had been put into the world merely to give pleasure to a man and to bear children.

All this made me hate more than ever the Bey who had so casually sent me off to this terrible fate. But I would sometimes wonder if I was now sufficiently submissive for his taste.

I'd never bothered much with painting my face. Now I had to learn not only to make up my face and eyes in the exaggerated way that Moorish men expect to find in a whore, but also to paint and rouge not only my nipples but also my beauty lips and mound, and to outline them with kohl. It was all very shocking, but strangely beautiful.

I had to learn about the little sponges, unguents and douches that black eunuchs would use in the brothel to prevent us from conceiving, and the special doses that we would given, if our Masters did decide that we were to conceive, to limit morning sickness.

There was one exception to all our instructors being Negroes. Our dancing and singing teacher was an Arab woman. She would arrive every day with a little troop of musicians. First she would make us practice singing in the Arabic style - a style that made a woman sound childlike and which I hated.

Singing lesson over, she would take off her black shroud. Underneath she would be dressed as a native belly dancer, with numerous veils and gaudy diaphanous trousers and blouse, and covered in chains of little imitation gold coins that left her belly bare. She would strap little rows of bells to her ankles.

Then she would begin to dance - and very shocking it was. It was not only belly dancing that she taught us, but also dances miming frustration and capture, dances miming being chained to the floor and raped, and dances miming every conceivable sexual act. She would always start with her hands raised above her head with the backs of her palms touching. When she was belly dancing, her muscles would perform the most extraordinary movements and to my disgust she would end by miming a woman reaching a climax.

Often she would take off her pretty Turkish slippers and dance bare footed on the tiled floor. "Moorish men," she would say, "like to see a woman dancing bare footed in front of them."

She would always end her dances on on her knees, on all fours, her head to the floor - in the same position of servility that we had been taught to assume in front of a man.

Then we would have to strap rows of bells onto our ankles, and copy her. Our overseer was always there with his cane ready to correct any shy reluctance on our part. He would remove our virgins' chastity belts, so that he and our instructress could see better how we were doing - especially in the embarrassing belly dances.

At first I was hopeless, and I felt I would never be able to do it. But gradually, day by day, I was discovering muscles in my belly that I never knew existed. I could feel that I was becoming more graceful.

"Think of yourselves as helpless slaves," our Instructress would cry. "Only a girl who enjoys being belled and chained for her Master's delight can dance properly before a man. A slave girl is not allowed to speak to a Moorish man. She must arouse him through her dancing and movements. Only if he seizes you and flings you onto his couch, will you know that you have danced well."

She insisted that we be kept indoors as much as possible, so that our bodies became dead white. "The belly of a dancer must be soft and white," she would say.

To my shame, I could not help becoming aroused myself by all this. Indeed, during our dancing, Bashir Aga would go down the line of girls checking that each had become moist with her own arousal. It was all desperately humiliating, especially since if he found a girl was still quite dry, he would use his cane on her. To my utter shame I found this would immediately have the desired effect. It was as if I had an inbred and exciting reaction to being beaten.

With the enthusiastic teaching of our Instructress, aided by fear of the cane, we became less and less inhibited in our dancing. Looking at the big mirror on the wall, I was often amazed at the beautiful and licentious creature that I saw staring back at me as she writhed provocatively on the floor to the music, or stood erect with her hands above her head, palms touching, belly and breasts shaking and revolving erotically, before, accompanied by a crash of cymbals, she flung herself to the floor, hands outstretched, head looking up adoringly, in a gesture of utter submission.

And to think that this creature had been Miss Barbara Kennedy, a rather puritanical and out-spoken governess! The young woman who dared to smack the face of the Bey! What would he say if he saw me swaying and writhing to the music? Would I excite him? Would he want to seize me and rape me? Did I want that? I could not help looking up wistfully at the empty gallery.

Chapter 12

PAGE BOYS

It came as a great shock to me, a couple of weeks after we started our intensive training, to learn that as high class whores we would have to compete with white page boys.

Indeed we were now joined on most days by a class of newly enslaved boys, together with their two big Negress supervisors. Hassan Ali intended to sell them, like us, as trained brothel slaves, or as personal page boys, cup bearers or garzons.

I could not help thinking back, during those joint lessons, to Malta and to the Bey's own page boy. I began to feel jealous of him. He served the Bey all day and every day. Was I beginning to wish that I did too?

Except for belly dancing, these pretty young youths were given virtually the same training as ourselves, taught to make up their faces like a girl and to move like one. We were told that some Moorish high class brothels would offer their clients a choice of either white page boys or white slave girls - or both. With their long carefully brushed hair, painted lips, flashing eyes outlined in kohl and henna decorated buttocks they would be serious rivals for the attentions of the clients.

It was a rivalry that we would have to take seriously, as we would also have to take that of other girls, for we were warned that top class brothel owners did not have the space for a girl who was not pulling her weight. Any girl who did not earn a certain sum for her owner each week would be quickly sold on to one of the brothels that catered for sailors or the Pasha's black troops.

I don't know which found it more embarrassing, we women having to practice doing the most intimate and degrading things with our huge Negro trainers and with ourselves in front of these white youths, or the page boys having to do them in front of us white women. In both cases the whip ruled, for they were clearly as scared of their instructress' dog whips as we were of Bashir Aga's cane.

Both women and boys were often kept naked during our joint training classes. The youth's manhoods, in contrast to the huge ones of our black instructors, were soft and tiny.

I saw that, behind their manhoods, again in contrast to the large heavy sacks of the Negroes that I had been made to lick and caress, these white boys had just ... nothing, nothing at all. They had all apparently been freshly gelded.

Moslem men I had already learned were absorbed by the idea of power, power over women, and particularly over white Christian women, whom they really enjoyed debasing down to the level of animals. I now learned that they also enjoyed having power over boys, particularly white Christian boys, whom they castrated to ensure that they neither enjoyed nor displayed any manly feelings, especially when in attendance to their Master on his visits to the harem.

The boys were gradually acquiring many of the physical characteristics of girls with soft beardless skins, swelling hips and smaller waists - and in some cases, I was astonished to see, budding little breasts.

A month previously the mere idea of anything like this would have shocked and appalled me. It still did, but I had learned that it was something that I must accept as part of my new life as a slave girl.

I also learned that there was a world of difference between the ugly tough black eunuchs and these delicate white boy eunuchs. We women could have twisted the white boys round our fingers. That's why white eunuchs were not used to supervise slave girls, whereas black ones had been used in the Moslem world for terrifying and controlling white women for centuries.

It all seemed a long way from the simple life of Dermot in the green hills of the Emerald Isle.

Chapter 13

THE BEY AND THE BASTINADO

We had now been subjected to intensive training for about a month - though we had of course no way of counting the time, no calendars, no watches, no writing materials. I was a very different person to the angry, rather puritanical young woman who had been shipwrecked. I was now sexually aware. I knew how to attract and please men in the most degrading and shame-making ways. Thanks to Bashir's Aga's cane, I was now a trained whore.

Hassan Ali and his assistants used to come into the gallery every day to watch and discuss our progress. They would sit cross legged in comfort, in the Eastern way, whilst a team of page boys brought them delicious looking sherbets and sweetmeats. Then they would look down critically whilst we sweated and strained below.

One day Bashir Aga painted the last three figures of our slave numbers across our bellies in large Arabic numbers. A little later, Hassan Ali came into the gallery with his party whilst we were practising our belly dancing. Instantly the music stopped and we prostrated ourselves before him, our faces to the floor.

"Would you like to see them dance, my friend?" I heard Hassan Ali ask. "I think you will be surprised how much progress these sluts have made thanks to Bashir Aga's cane!"

"Yes, do please carry on."

It was the voice of the Bey! My heart missed several beats.

The musicians started up again. Our dancing instructress clapped her hands. Quickly we stood up and with the backs of our hands touching above our head, resumed our belly dancing.

We were dressed only in transparent trousers which had been cut away in front to bare our quivering beauty lips. We virgins had had our chastity belts removed for this lesson. I blushed deeply at the thought of what the handsome Irishman must be looking at. But then I was carried away with the music and by having to concentrate on the steps and movements we had been taught.

I gave a quick glance up towards the gallery and saw that the Bey was sitting to one side. He was watching me. I smiled back and swayed and wriggled towards him as provocatively as I could. I flashed my eyes up at him in the way that I had to practice in the big wall mirror. I shook my breasts in the way that I had been taught. I could feel my nipples becoming erect with excitement, and of course I wriggled my belly like mad. I could feel my inner body reacting as well.

I should be hating him, I told myself, not lusting after him! I longed to call out to him, to call him a swine, to curse him, to ... but of course I did not dare do any of these things.

Then suddenly I behaved like a little child. I put my tongue out at him and made a face to show my contempt.

Instantly there was chaos. Hassan Ali clapped his hands. The musicians stopped. The class froze.

"That slut," shouted Hassan Ali, pointing at my cringing figure, "has just insulted my guest."

I felt my neck being gripped by a furious Bashir Aga, livid at his demonstration of control over us being wrecked by my impetuous gesture. He flung me to the ground. Hastily I licked the floor and opened my legs as placatory gesture, appalled at what I had done, but it was too late.

"What punishment would make up for the slight on your honour?" I heard the desperately embarrassed Hassan Ali formally ask the Bey.

"Oh, it is no great matter. The bastinado would be sufficient," replied the Bey.

The bastinado! Oh no! Once again my hot Irish temper had got me into serious trouble with the Bey. Would I never learn?

"I would not want to spoil her undoubted dancing talent for too long," the hateful voice continued languidly. "Fifteen strokes should be sufficient."

The whole class gasped. Fifteen strokes of the bastinado! But Louise, our head girl, gave a little chuckle of satisfaction. She hated me. I hated her more than ever.

"Very well, Your Excellency," Hassan Ali said in an ingratiating voice. "Now continue the dancing!"

The music became faster and faster. We were supposed to be swaying and wriggling as we mimed a girl reaching a climax. But I could hardly concentrate on what I was supposed to be doing. Fifteen strokes of the bastinado! Of the bastinado!

With a sudden crash, the music stopped. The entire class flung itself down, faces to the ground and arms outstretched, making a pretty picture of utter subservience.

There was a long pause, as if Hassan Ali was making up his mind about something.

"Yes," he said, evidently talking to his assistants as well as to the Bey, "they are coming on well."

For a whole day I had been frightened out of my wits at the thought of what was to come. I had never seen a girl being bastinadoed. But I had heard terrifying stories about it. How I hated the Bey for having so casually condemned me to it for what was, after all, little more than a prank.

That evening we were paraded. In front of us was a low wooden stocks with two holes in it. The actual stocks were hinged so that something could be placed in the holes and the top brought down to hold them there.

I was called forward, trembling with fear. I was told to take off my tunic, lest I wet it with the pain. I was told to lie down on my back. My ankles were raised and imprisoned in the stocks.

"For impertinence to a Master, fifteen strokes," Bashir Aga intoned. "You call out number of each stroke!"

He raised his cane high in the air. It was a heavier cane than his normal thin whippy one.

"In the name of Allah the Merciful, the only True God."

I clenched my toes. I could hear the rest of the class catch their breath. The Negro brought his cane hard down across the delicate soles of my feet. It was like a streak of fire. The pain was appalling. I screamed my hatred of the Bey, that swine of a renegade Irishman who was just as cruel to women as his awful Turkish employers.

"In the name of Allah, the Merciful, the only True God." Seconds later I was screaming my heart out again. Oh how I hated this Negro and how I hated the Bey!

Two more strokes were delivered amidst screams from me. Then there was a pause.

Only four strokes! Another eleven to come. How could I possibly survive them?

I saw the Negro bow in the direction of the little gallery. I saw all the class fall down onto their knees, their heads to the ground. Turning awkwardly on my back, I tried to see up to the gallery.

Then I saw him. The Bey!

He was sitting comfortably on the ottoman. His page boy was kneeling in front of him, holding up a tray of sweetmeats and sherbets. I saw the Bey put one of the

95

sweetmeats into his mouth and casually take a sip from a glass. He was casually drinking, and a woman was being bastinadoed, at his request, at his feet!

I heard his slow drawling voice.

"Do please carry on. The slut certainly does seem to be making an awful lot of noise. I do like to hear a woman screaming properly when she gets the bastinado. Then you know she won't misbehave like that again. There's nothing I detest so much as an impertinent white woman who is too big for her boots."

So I was really being punished for what happened in Malta, for arguing with him in public and for then smacking his face. Oh how he was enjoying getting his revenge!

"Master," I screamed out in English, "I'm sorry! I'm sorry for insulting you in Malta. I'm sorry!"

I could hear the intake of breath from the class. I heard a snort of fury from the Negro. But I had apologised. I had said I was sorry. Surely he would now tell Bashir Aga to release me, and allow me to crawl crying to his feet?

"Two extra strokes, I think," came that languid, arrogant voice.

"Oh no! No!" I screamed, but my scream was cut short by four more strokes in quick succession, that left me panting and sobbing my heart out.

"I think we'll take the remaining nine strokes nice and slowly," came the hated voice. I strained to peer up at him again. He was smiling and sipping his sherbet as if my flogging was just a little amusement. Oh, how I hated him. And yet I could feel that there was a strange bond between a woman who had been beaten in front of a man, and that man himself.

The Negro made me kiss the cane. The next stroke was gentler.

"You tell Master you happy he order bastinado for you. Tell you deserve bastinado."

I knew when I was beaten. At that moment I would have done anything, said anything, to stop the terrible thrashing.

"Your Excellency, Sir," I cried out in Lingua Franca, "I deserved to be beaten. Thank you for having me beaten in front of you." I really felt utterly abject, utterly subservient. "I am not worthy to lick the dirt off your shoes."

There was a pause.

"I love you! I love you, Sir!" I cried out in English.

The awful thing was that I really meant it - such is the power of the cane on a young woman.

But the Bey ignored my cry. He nodded to Bashir Aga to continue my slowly drawn out punishment.

The next ten minutes were quite unbelievable terrible.

Suddenly, when I was almost out of my mind with pain, I felt our black overseer unfasten my ankles. I could not stand from the pain. I fell to my knees before the little gallery, sobbing in abject humility before the Bey. Without any prompting I kissed the floor in front of him, carefully and slowly. Then I raised my head slightly, hoping to see a little gesture of compassion, but he had already gone.

Would I ever see him again? I had cried out the truth - that I loved him. He wasn't even interested!

The pain was terrible. I still could not stand. Driven on by Bashir Aga's terrible cane, I had to crawl somehow to my cage. I broke down and sobbed my heart out. Bashir Aga was grinning from ear to ear as he locked the metal grill at the front of the cage.

Chapter 14

SENT TO MARKET

All the class was in an uproar after a casual remark by our Master that the best of us were going to be sent to market next week, with the remainder, 'second class girls', being sent as one or two job lots to country brothel owners. The culmination of the long hours of humiliating training was about to be reached. We going to be sold! Sold like animals in a market! But which would be chosen for which? Which of us was better than the others?

Meanwhile our classes and instruction continued without respite. We were now taught the slave movements that the auctioneer might decide to order us to assume under his orders in the auction ring or which Bashir Aga would order in the examination room. They were intended to be degrading for us, but stimulating for the buyers.

We had to learn a complex series of different positions, each intended to show off our bodies in a different and exciting way, and to hint at the pleasures that we had been taught to give. Each position, whether it was standing bent over with our legs wide apart, kneeling up with our bodies straining back and our knees wide apart, or lying on our backs with one leg raised, had to be assumed with a graceful gesture and held for several seconds before moving to the next one.

We each had to learn to make a different and striking entrance into the auction ring or sales room, so as to attract the attention of the jaded brothel owners. Isabella had to practice walking up and down as if showing off a beautiful dress, despite being stark naked. Another had to enter doing an erotic belly dance, her breasts swinging wildly.

As for me, for the first few days my poor feet were still too painful from the bastinado, but then gradually I had to practice entering at a fast run, running with my knees raised high in the air, and my manacled hands clasped behind my neck.

I felt very foolish doing this, but I could see that it would make an amusing and arousing sight for a man thinking of buying me. Buying me! Oh my God! What sort of man was going to buy me and what sort of brothel would he put me in? All the Moorish men I had seen had seemed to be cruel swine who enjoyed debasing white women and who certainly didn't care about their feelings.

At night I would weep with fear and trepidation at the thought of what was going to happen to me. Oh, if only I had not insulted the Bey in Malta and smacked his face in public! If only he had rescued me from Hassan Ali's terrifying slave training school and sent me back to Malta. If only, indeed, he had taken me for his own harem, for his own collection of European concubines! Goodness, how exciting that would have been! He was so masterful, so strong minded, so decisive, so wonderful. It must be thrilling to be in his harem, in his power ... in his bed!

Then suddenly one morning we were all lined up. We were wearing our tunics. Bashir Aga had a pile of leather objects. He came up to me first - he knew I was a potential trouble maker. His boy assistant held my chained hands tightly, whilst he himself picked up something from the pile and thrust a ball of leather into my mouth. Attached to the front of the ball was a strap, which he fastened tightly behind my neck. The ball filled my mouth, forcing my tongue down and keeping my mouth wide open. I could only make little moaning noises.

I shook my head and struggled to free my hands, but to no avail. The burly Negro slipped a hood over my head. I was in complete darkness, except for two little breathing holes low down near my nose and could see nothing. I felt him fasten the bottom of the hood to the strap behind my neck, heard the click of a small padlock.

At the same time I felt him fasten two heavy chains to my collar.

The hateful black boy let go of my hands. Desperately I tore at the hood and tried to pull it off. I twisted and turned. Then I found the unyielding padlock and heard the Negro boy laugh.

I tried to scream, but the leather ball reduced my yells to little grunts. Slowly I quietened down as I realised that I was not going to suffocate.

I heard other girls being similarly gagged and hooded. I was pushed backwards and felt girls on either side of me. I heard my collar chains being fastened to their collars, and other similar noises.

I stood there chained and unable to see or speak. Terrified I wondered what was going to happen.

Suddenly my collar was jerked by the chain leading to the girl on my right. A whip cracked. No order was given, but I was now well enough trained to know that I must quickly stumble after the girl, dragging the girl on my left behind me. Shuffling along I felt that that we were being lead out of the building in which we had been virtually imprisoned for so long. There was sand beneath my bare feet.

What was happening? I could see nothing. I shivered as I wondered if we were one of the job lots being sent to a country brothel. Again I was terrified.

I felt my lead chain go slack. I stopped. Again no orders were given. We were well broken in.

"Strip!" It was the voice of Bashir Aga. Again there was a crack of a whip. I put my chained wrists up to the shoulders of my tunic and undid the buttons. I felt the tunic slip to my ankles. I stepped out of it and bent down to pick it up, as we had been taught, and held it out in front of me as I heard the black eunuch coming down the line. He took my tunic, came behind me and removed my chastity belt. Then he went on down the line and I relaxed.

Suddenly I heard the swish of a cane. I felt a line of fire across my calves. I cried out behind my gag.

"You stand up properly, Number 632!" shouted the Negro's assistant, giving me another stroke across my calves. It was excruciating.

It was awful to be disciplined by a mere boy, a black boy. But, hastily, I raised my hooded head. I thrust out my naked breasts. I thrust forward my beauty lips. I wondered if any men, Moorish or Negro, were watching. My knees were prudishly pressed together. Quickly I parted my legs and bent my knees. I did not want another stroke of the cane for not showing respect.

"Down on all fours! All of you!"

Quickly I knelt down, hating being treated in this offhand way. How the Negroes enjoyed doing it.

"Crawl up!"

A tug on my collar - I crawled up a wooden ramp. It had wooden slats to allow animals to get a better grip. I was thrust into something. I felt other girls in the coffle being thrust into it. I was pushed along to make more room. I felt straw on the floor - under it were iron bars. I put my chained wrists up above my head and felt more iron bars, then heard the crash of a cage door being closed, then bolts being drawn across and locked. I felt the cage suddenly sway and heard the creak of wheels and the crack of a whip. So the cage was clearly mounted on a cart. We were being taken to ... to market to be sold? ... or to the interior as a job lot?

The cart seemed to be moving faster than the ox-drawn waggon that had brought me here. I guessed that it was being drawn by mules. Suddenly it stopped.

"Mahmud! Come on! Get your girls into the cage!" It was the hated voice of Bashir Aga, speaking in Lingua Franca. I had noticed how the Negroes tended to speak to each in broken Lingua Franca and to their Masters in Arabic. They used only Lingua Franca to the white women in their charge, of course, and presumably found it easier than Arabic. "How many you got this time?"

"Three." Mahmud's voice was high pitched like that of Bashir Aga. Evidently Hassan Ali liked to use black eunuchs to train his white women slaves.

"Well, hurry up. I not want wait all day for your useless cast offs."

"They not useless. They all good milk yielders. They fetch better prices than your skinny creatures."

I heard the clinking of an approaching chained coffle, and the crack of a whip.

"Stay down!" It was the voice of Mahmud.

There was the creak of the cage door being opened, then the noise of a stick against the bars.

"Go in, my beauties. Go on! Crawl along, crawl along!"

I felt buxom bodies brushing past me. I put out my hands and touched hooded heads and manacled wrists - just like my own. I heard little moaning whimpers - evidently they were gagged just like us. Then I touched a breast. It seemed huge, as it hung down. Suddenly I realised who they were and the significance of Mahmud's talk of good yielders. They had come from Hassan Ali's 'dairy herd'. I remembered how my friend Carlotta had been selected for it, after being made to crawl round and round to show off her breasts.

A few minutes later the cart stopped again.

"What's for market, Zalu?" I heard Bashir Aga ask.

"Six of my best!" replied Zalu. "For white girls they very strong now, carry heavy loads and work long hours.

102

But not needed here now. New batch of women come for field training."

So we were being taken to market in Marsa, and not sent off inland. I had been judged to be one of the best girls. I was a best whore!

"You had heads shorn! Lucky you. I wish I could do that with my women," I heard Bashir Aga say enviously. "You get good price?".

"Yes, good demand still in Europe for genuine European girls hair, even though wigs now going out of fashion. And Hassan Ali allow me keep money from hair as little present."

Soon another coffle of hooded and manacled women crawled into the crowded cage. I felt a sharp dig from a pointed stick. "Go on! Move up!"

I heard a cover of some sort being drawn over the cage and fastened down at the sides, and soon we were off - but off to where?

The day was getting on. Crowded under the cover of the cage we were all sweating. Then I smelt the distinctive smells of an Eastern town and began to hear many voices. We were entering a town, presumably Marsa itself. The voices became louder. They were men's voices, apparently shouting their rival wares or raised in anger and dispute. These were not the falsetto voices of eunuchs but the deep voices of real men, Moorish men, frightening and demanding men. I gave a little shiver of fear. They were not speaking in Lingua Franca, but in Arabic, a language of which we were deliberately ignorant.

Then I heard the noise of a gate being opened. The voices grew more remote. The gate was apparently being closed behind us. Silence. The cart stopped. We had arrived.

PART THREE
SOLD

Chapter 15

THE NIGHT BEFORE THE SALE

I heard the cage door being unlocked. One by one the three hooded coffles were drawn out of the cage by their black overseers. We had to walk down a sort of ramp, still chained to each other by the neck.

I felt I was treading on cobblestones, and soon I heard men's voices. Real men, Arabs, the type of men we had been taught to please. I felt myself blushing under the hood, for I was naked.

Then I heard our eunuch coming down the line taking off our stifling hoods. He unlocked the hood and lifted it off, leaving only the gag. Thankfully I took a breath of fresh air and shook my hair, blinking in the sunlight.

Hesitantly I glanced around, keeping my head bent. We were in a large courtyard. I was rather glad to see that my friend Isabella was one of the coffle. We exchanged a nervous smile. I longed to hold her hand, but we were separated by two girls on the coffles. I longed to ask her what she thought was happening, but she was also still gagged.

The courtyard was surrounded by buildings on three sides and by high walls on the other. Round the courtyard were rows of low cages and pens filled with sheep and goats. No! To my horror I saw that some of the cages contained naked women - white women. Gripping the bars, they were kneeling on all fours and peering out at us silently. Each wore a gag like mine.

In front of us was a cattle dipping trough of red coloured water. There were bars over the top of the trough to prevent a frightened animal in the trough from climbing out.

Wooden railings led in a V-shaped tunnel to the end of the trough nearest us. It was like a cattle crush, but with bars over the top as well. It led to a wooden platform over the end of the trough.

At the other end of the trough were more barred tunnels that could be adjusted to lead to one of the various pens and cages. Once an animal was in the system it could be driven into the appropriate cage or pen. Indeed, behind the railings, and by the trough, were several half naked Negroes with pointed canes like those used to drive cattle. Two well dressed Arabs were directing operations. It was their voices that I had heard.

The Negroes were poking their pointed canes through the bars to drive some goats along the V-shaped tunnel. As each goat stepped onto the wooden platform, a Negro would pull a lever, and the platform would collapse, throwing the animal into the trough. It was obviously deep, for the goats would disappear momentarily under the water and emerge swimming along the trough, anxious to reach the far end. As they did so, they would climb up a ramp under the water. Then the Negroes, again poking their sticks through the bars of the tunnel, would drive them into a pen.

Being dipped in the pen was evidently a health requirement for animals. I had seen a similar arrangement at a sheep market in Ireland.

The last goat was dropped into the trough, swam along it and was driven into a pen.

One of the Arabs turned to our eunuch. He pointed at our coffle of naked gagged women and then at the trough. I could not believe it. We too were to be dipped!

I longed to call out, to protest, to scream for help, to shout out that we were respectable European women, and that I was a British subject. But, of course, like all the women in the courtyard, I was still gagged.

Bashir Aga drove our coffle up the V-shaped tunnel towards the trough. I was terrified. The girl in front of me fell into the trough with a splash as the wooden platform opened under her. As she did so, I found myself pulled by my neck chain onto the platform. I saw the hideous grinning face of a Negro pulling a lever, and a second later I was spluttering behind my gag in the foul tasting water.

I struggled with my feet to find the bottom of the trough, but it was too deep. The pull on my neck chain from the girl ahead of me was dragging me along the trough, but I was slowed by the pull from the girl behind me in the coffle. Halfway along I saw another Negro. As I came level with him he put his boot down onto my fingers, which were desperately gripping the side of the trough, making me let go. Then he bent down and pushed my head under the horrible red liquid again. I struggled, but he held my head under the water. Just when I thought I would drown he let me go, and once again I rose sputtering to the surface. I had been well and truly dipped!

Seconds later I felt the bottom of the trough beneath my feet. Dripping wet, I found myself crawling along another tunnel, behind the girl ahead of me, towards a small cage.

Soon six soaking wet women, still gagged and chained by the neck to each other, were kneeling on the straw covered floor of the low cage, gripping the bars with manacled hands. Our black overseer closed the heavy bolts on the door to our cage and locked them. He wrote something in chalk on a blackboard attached to the bars, then walked away.

It was now the turn of the coffle of six field slaves to be put though the dip. They were strong looking girls, who would be sold largely for their strength rather than their looks. Their heads had recently been shaved and were quite smooth and shiny, giving them a strangely inhuman look. I remembered what their eunuch had said about selling their hair and shivered. It might have happened to me.

We were now left for several hours in our cage, just looking at each other and unable to speak.

Bashir Aga eventually came back carrying a bucket of slave gruel and a medicine bottle. One by one we had to stick our heads out through a small feeding trap door in the front of the cage.

When it was my turn, he unlocked the fastening of my gag at the back of my neck, and gave me a spoonful of the tasteless slave gruel. I was longing to take advantage of the gag being removed to ask him where we were and what was going to happen to us, but one look at his cane stopped me from daring to speak without permission. I just eagerly swallowed up my feed. I was hungry after the long journey and the terrifying episode in the cattle dip.

Then, gripping me tightly by the nose, he forced me to swallow a large spoonful of the strange medicine, stroking my throat to make sure that I swallowed it all. Then he re-fastened my gag. He patted my belly approvingly through the bars, before thrusting me back into the cage and pulling up the next girl by her collar chain.

It was getting dark. To protect us against the cold night air, our Negro overseer dropped a cover down over the front of the cage. The body heat of so many women in the small cage would keep us warm - as it had in the waggon after I was captured.

Chapter 16

PREPARED FOR SALE

Next morning our Negro overseer came and called us one by one to the front of the cage and checked the effect of the awful purge - which is what that strange medicine had turned out to be. Later I was to learn that it was normal to sell a white woman with an empty belly lest she might soil herself and the block on which she was she auctioned or displayed.

These blocks were covered in sawdust, but this was more for psychological reasons than as a precaution against the worst happening. As I was soon to learn for myself, a girl feels the sawdust under her naked feet, and this has a powerful effect in making her realise that she is just being treated as an animal - which is all she is in the eyes of her Moorish masters.

When the horrible black eunuch was satisfied that each of us had indeed emptied herself, he let us out of the cage, removed our gags and gave us a a handful of cattle food, saying that this was all that we would get that day. We were also given a small drink of water, again limited for fear we might lose control of ourselves later on.

We were then taken into a large room with a big bath and mirrors on the walls. It was rather like the room to which we had first been taken to beautify ourselves before being looked at by Hassan Ali and his henchmen - and by the Irish Bey, I remembered, with a shudder - or was it a sigh?

There were sweet smelling soaps, heavily scented Eastern oils and unguents, brushes and combs. There was rouge for our cheeks, nipples and body lips, kohl for outlining our eyes, nipples and intimacies, henna to decorate our bellies and the palms of our hands - all the things we had been taught to do in the Moorish fashion during our training.

Bashir Aga stood over us as we gratefully washed in the bath and then titivated and painted our faces and our bodies. One by one, we had to climb onto a couch and lie on our backs with our legs wide apart and our arms raised, whilst the burly Negro, armed with tweezers and burning depilatory creams, inspected us for the slightest sign of body hair, even turning us over onto our bellies for a check from behind.

I had been taught that Moorish men like a young woman to look like a little girl and to behave like one - often even dressing their concubines, especially their white ones, like little girls, making them play with dolls and sleep in cots, not only under the eye of his black eunuchs, but also under the supervision of a bustling black nanny. Some brothels catered for this, and we had been taught to lisp whenever a Master spoke to us.

Another group of white women, apparently from another slave dealer, were being similarly prepared by their black eunuch overseer. We could not help regarding them with a mixture of jealousy and scorn. They were not nearly so beautiful or well trained as us! We had been taught to move much more gracefully and excitingly than them!

The three milk slaves were also present, having their large breasts painted with henna and their nipples with kohl. It made them look very erotic.

Even the field slaves were brought in to be beautified. Their black overseer began running his razor over their strange looking bald heads and then polishing the skin until it gleamed above their kohl-ringed flashing eyes.

"This feel smooth like satin," said their overseer to ours with a grin. "Better than your hairy lot!"

"Bah! Your women move like oxen - mine move like little fluttering birds!" replied Bashir Aga. I felt a little thrill of pride at his words.

I remembered that although a buyer of field slaves would mainly be interested in their strength and stamina, he would also want to use them for his own pleasure, and probably put them at the disposal of his black overseers.

When Bashir Aga was at last satisfied with our appearance, he produced a pile of beautiful blue and white ribbons and satin bows. Blue and white were the distinctive colours of Hassan Ali's slave training establishment. He fastened one bow round each of our necks, just below our heavy brass collars, and another high up round our right thighs.

Then he tied a short blue and white stiff frilly skirt round our waists, with a big bow in the small of our backs. The skirt was only about six inches long and was heavily starched so that it stuck out sideways, leaving our bellies and intimacies bare and well displayed.

I was shocked to see in the mirror how erotic and exciting they made me. I looked at a pregnant milk girl, who had been dealt with the same way. They showed off her swelling belly, making her look even more heavily pregnant.

Still chained by the neck, and of course with our wrists still manacled, Bashir Aga led our coffle into a large adjoining hall. It seemed to be a sort of exhibition hall. Down one side were stalls containing beautiful Arab horses being carefully groomed until their coats gleamed. Another line of stalls contained donkeys and mules. There was also a line of pens containing sheep and goats: there was a strong animal smell. Down the other side were doors that apparently led out into the street. On the other side was a smaller door with a series of collecting pens in front of it.

Behind a roped off section of the large hall, guarded by an armed Negro, were several lines of small stone platforms, covered with a sprinkling of sawdust. Each was about three foot square and set several feet above the floor. Several were already occupied by women. Our overseer unshackled us one by one from the coffle, and made us climb up onto one of the platforms, and then fastened our collar chain to a ring in the centre of the platforms.

Isabella was chained to the platform next to mine. We were all in a little group, so that he could keep an eye on us.

An elderly Moor came up and spoke to Bashir Aga. He was carrying some instruments and several bowls. He pulled out a sheaf of papers and began to discuss them with our overseer, pointing at us.

He came up to me. I began to tremble. Bashir Aga gripped me by the hair and pulled my head back to hold me still. The Moor picked up my forearm. He checked the slave number tattooed there against his papers. Then he pulled my left breast forward. I saw he had a small brush in his hand. I felt him painting something on my breast just above the nipple. Then he went behind me and repeated the process on my right buttock.

"Lot Number," murmured Bashir Aga. "You thirty six."

The Negro pulled my hair back even more, forcing me to arch my back, as I knelt, still on all fours. I felt the elderly Moor's hands part my body lips. I tried to wriggle away, but Bashir Aga held me quite still. I felt the Moor's finger probing up inside me. I gave a gasp of protest. He was checking my virginity!

Apparently satisfied, he withdrew his finger. He came round in front of me. I saw him mark his papers. He wrote out a certificate and pasted it on the front of my platform. I felt so ashamed.

111

The Moor nodded at Bashir Aga, who now pushed my head down so that I was looking down at the top of my platform. I saw the Moor pour some water into one of the smaller bowls until it was completely full. He placed an empty larger bowl under my hanging right breast. Then, whilst Bashir Aga again held me quite still, he carefully immersed my right breast fully into the smaller bowl. The displaced water splashed down into the larger bowl. He took away the larger bowl, and with some portable scales began to weigh it.

Suddenly I realised what the clever Moor was doing. I remembered being taught that Archimedes had said that the weight of a floating object was equal to the weight of water it displaced. Since the human body more or less floated in water, by immersing my breast and weighing the water it displaced, he had weighed my breast! Indeed I saw him writing it down on his papers and on the certificate he had pasted onto the front of my platform.

Now not only had my virginity been certified, but also the weight of my breasts. I felt more like an animal than ever, as I knelt chained on the sawdust.

I saw the six bald-headed field slaves being chained to another set of platforms in a part of the hall clearly set aside for field slaves. They were kept standing, however - presumably so that their muscles could be more easily be assessed. By each of their platforms was a heavy weighted bar, which I saw them being made to practice picking up and holding up high above their heads, to show off their strength.

I saw other field slaves being brought in and similarly chained. Many of them were older women, well tanned by years of toiling in the sun, and now pregnant as proof of their fertility.

"Pay attention!" barked our black overseer. "In a few minutes, doors opened. Men come now to inspect."

As he paused to let his words sink in, several of the girls started to sob. The big Negro tapped his whip angrily against the palm of his hand.

"Silence! Try look attractive and try catch attention of buyers from brothels. You smile, look happy. You look ahead whilst he feels you. You only speak if man wants to hear your voice. Count to ten. You slave girls not supposed to be clever enough to count higher. Understand?"

"Yes, Sir," we chorused dutifully like a class of little girls.

"And if you told to jump, you stand up quickly and start jumping up and down with hands behind neck. You go on until I say stop. I watching you all. Any woman sulky or bad tempered get thrashing of her life!"

"Yes, Sir," we chorused nervously. We had practised all this so often during our training. Now it was for real.

"Then you make sure you show off well in auction ring. You not get another chance tomorrow. Tomorrow for boys. If not sold go back Hassan Ali's estate for bastinado." I shivered with fear. The Bastinado! Even the word made every a slave girl scared stiff. I would do anything, absolutely anything, rather than risk being given the bastinado again.

Chapter 17

EXAMINED IN THE EXHIBITION HALL

The doors leading into the market were flung open and I had my first glimpse of Marsa.

All I could see were white painted flat roofed houses, with trellised windows reaching up for several stories, and, down in the narrow streets, numerous Arab men, wearing robes of every colour from immaculate white to gold edged black. Some wore richly embroidered turbans, others red felt fezes, and others Arab headdress.

It was the first time I had seen large numbers of rich Moorish men - the men in whose hands my fate now lay. They were dignified, calm and well dressed, as they stepped into the exhibition hall of the market. Many were attended by white page boys. Many had brought their black eunuchs with them to examine the women on offer. They seemed corpulent and prosperous men who walked slowly and ponderously.

Some were more interested in the Arab horses than in women. Some, clearly farmers and landowners, seemed equally divided between the donkeys and the field slaves. Some, often rather elderly, seemed more interested in the milk slaves. Only a small number of rather cruel looking men were allowed into the roped-off area that contained us trained brothel slaves.

These men walked past my little platform talking amongst themselves, occasionally pointing to a particular woman who had caught their eye, and then going up for a closer look.

I saw that across the hall, Hassan Ali's bald headed field slaves were attracting a large crowd. The blue and white decorated women were being made to lift up the heavy weights and to hold them up above their heads, as they struggled and sweated, whilst eager Moorish hands felt their straining thigh muscles to judge how well they would pull a plough or turn an irrigation wheel. Other hands would be feeling between their parted legs, examining them intimately to judge their breeding capacity. I was shocked at the callous way the Moors treated white women with no more respect than they would an animal.

Suddenly I heard a voice near me, speaking in Lingua Franca to our overseer. It was normal for the Moors to speak to Negroes in Lingua Franca, for many Negroes had difficulty in speaking Arabic.

"Number 632! Position for inspection!" It was the moment of truth. A hideous repulsively fat Moor was going to feel me, probably a brothel owner who was going to assess my capability of earning him large sums of money as a whore. Despite all my training I felt desperately embarrassed and ashamed. Would I ever be able to hold my head up again in Ireland? Would I ever be able to look Dermot in the eye the again after this?

"Head up! Not look round!"

Quickly I assumed the position I knew so well. The weeks of training overcame my nervousness and I tried to keep my eyes fixed on the wall ahead.

I felt a warm podgy hand on my thigh, feeling my dancing muscles. He ran his hand down my leg. Then he ran it up my back. He came in front of me, made me open my mouth, pulled down my lower lip, examined my teeth. I longed to bite his hand, but I was too scared. He bent down and smelt my breath. He was revolting. He put down both his hands to feel my breasts, looking down at the certificate of their weight, and then testing the sensitivity of my nipples. I could not help squirming, and he looked pleased.

Then I had to kneel up. A small crowd collected as he carefully examined each breast. He felt my belly and my arms.

I had to kneel down again on all fours, this time with my head to the floor of the platform. As I had been taught, I kept my back straight and my legs wide apart, thrusting back to give him a more intimate view.

I was deeply embarrassed with so many men standing around me and even more when I felt my beauty lips being roughly parted. I winced. Was he also going to test my virginity? But instead of inserting his finger and probing, he ran his fingers up and down in an experienced way and then began to tickle my beauty bud. To my shame I felt myself begin to wriggle in time to the Moor's loathsome caresses. I heard the watching men laugh, and blushed deeply.

He took his hand away. Thinking that he had finished, I looked round - he was dipping his fingers deep into a pot of animal grease that I had noticed on each platform.

"Head down! Not dare look round! I not warn you again!" bawled Bashir Aga, giving me a sharp tap across the shoulders with his cane.

Quickly I put my head down again to the sawdust and straightened my back. I felt my buttocks being parted.

"Oh!" I cried. I had not expected to be examined there. The watching men laughed.

I heard the Moor say something to Bashir Aga. I heard the Negro reply: "She not stretched."

Suddenly I was penetrated by a grease covered finger, deeply penetrated. I gave a little cry. "Keep still!" ordered the Negro, probing even deeper. No wonder we had been given the strong purge the night before! Satisfied he withdrew his finger.

116

He slapped my buttocks approvingly, as a man might affectionately slap the hindquarters of a favourite mare, then reached down and took hold of my left breast. He took careful note of my Lot Number. Then he strode off to have a look at Isabella, leaving me overwhelmed with shame and humiliation. No man had ever handled me so intimately and so callously. And he was so ugly!

A few minutes a skinny looking Arab with a straggly beard came up and spoke to Bashir Aga, pointing at me.

"Stand up!" shouted the Negro. "Jump!"

It was degrading having to do so in front of so many men, for the sight of my breasts bouncing up and down high above the crowd soon brought more men back to my platform. Perhaps that was the idea.

Soon I was getting out of breath, but Bashir Aga raised his cane warningly and I had to force myself to go on and on, jumping up and down, whilst the men pointed and laughed.

At last I was allowed to stop. But I had attracted the attention of several buyers, and there followed a long session of being kneaded, pummelled and felt all over by a series of hard faced men, notebooks in hand, or on their behalf by their black eunuchs.

Half an hour later, there was a sudden hush as a tall Negro, wearing a rich brocade robe, edged with fur, and a white conical felt hat, strode into the roped off section of the exhibition hall.

"Prepare to show subservience to the Pasha's chief black eunuch!" ordered our own black eunuch, raising his cane warningly. Obviously the Pasha's chief black eunuch was a very important man.

"Down!" shouted Bashir Aga. Moving as one, already on all fours, we obediently all lowered our heads to the floor of our platforms, our chained wrists now clasped behind our necks.

"I see you haven't lost your touch, Bashir Aga!" The Pasha's black eunuch laughed, his voice high pitched.

They were talking in Lingua Franca, perhaps for our benefit - though I was knew that black eunuchs were so used to speaking to their white charges in that simple language that they tended to use it amongst themselves as well. "What have these white sluts been sent to market as?"

"They are to be sold as trained whores - to brothel owners. And, Allah be praised, they have turned out really well. Look at them!" He turned to us and called out, "Prepare to kneel up, little bitches! ... Up!"

Again as one, we all knelt up straight on our platforms, keeping our eyes looking straight ahead, our knees well apart, and our chained wrists still clasped behind our necks.

"Don't they move well!" said Bashir Aga. "As a team they could put your revered Master into a very good temper!"

I felt the eyes of the other black eunuch on me. I was being assessed by an experienced judge of female flesh. I could not help feeling proud of my naked beauty and of my now more docile character.

"Yes, but my Master has enough white concubines at present. And any way he prefers a girl to enter his harem still relatively innocent and then to be specially trained to satisfy his particular needs. What he wants now is simply a couple of white milk slaves."

He left us and strolled over to the platforms of the milk slaves. I saw him feeling their breasts carefully, squeezing a little milk from each one to test how easy it would be for his Master to drink from her. They had not been milked since they left Hassan Ali's estate and their breasts were heavy with milk.

I saw him also examine the girl who had not yet foaled, to use the word that the Moors so humiliating used when referring to their white slave women. Not only was he carefully weighing her breasts in his hands, but he was also feeling her distended belly, before going behind her, as she knelt on all fours, feeling her beauty lips and her hips - and evidently judging whether or not she would deliver easily.

How awful, I thought, to be examined like that by a rich man's black eunuch. But I could I see that the girl was tremulously smiling at him, obviously pleased that she had caught the eye of such an important man. I saw the black eunuch nod and note down the girl's Lot Number.

I could not help feeling jealous. In a few hours she might be incarcerated in the Pasha's harem, waiting in luxury for her mulatto child to be born and taken away, so that she could then devote herself to supplying her Master with fresh milk. Whereas I would be incarcerated in some awful brothel.

My thoughts were interrupted, as I again knelt on all fours whilst being examined by a couple of dreadful Moors, by the sight of a tall good looking man in Turkish uniform striding across the hall in the direction of the horses. The Bey! Out of the corner of my eye, I saw him catch sight of Bashir Aga, and come across towards him.

My brain was in a turmoil. How awful to be seen being intimately inspected like this - seen by the man to whom I had last cried out, under the terrible bastinado, that I loved him. I could hear that arrogant voice greeting other men - apparently oblivious of the naked women being displayed around him.

I longed to turn and smile at him. I loved him! But, terrified of another application of the bastinado for being too forward, I kept my eyes fixed rigidly ahead.

I heard his voice from behind me. Despite myself, I felt myself strain to part my thighs even wider to catch his eye. Like a bitch on heat trying to attract the attention of the dog, I found myself wriggling my beauty lips in his direction. I felt bitterly ashamed, but it was better than risking the bastinado.

"You seem to have trained this slut very well!" I heard his voice still from behind me. "I'm sure she'll sell well. Now I must go and see the horses."

He left me flushed, aroused and desperately disappointed as the two hideous Moors, delighted by my excited state, re-commenced their probing examination. I longed to be ordered to stand up and jump, so that I might catch another glimpse of him across the hall. But those two damned Moors took their time with my intimacies, and by the time they ordered me to be jumped, the Bey was nowhere to be seen.

I almost sobbed with disappointment. Would I ever see him again? Even if, as I now realised, he would never have rescued me from slavery, he might have acquired me for his own harem - if only I had not so stupidly insulted him in Malta.

By now it was afternoon. The exhibition hall emptied, with the men presumably going back to their private harems or brothels for their siesta. For an hour Bashir Aga let us rest, curled up on our little platforms. We were not allowed to eat anything, but we were given a little sweet sherbet to drink.

Then our overseer came down the line of kneeling women with a bucket of water and a sponge. He washed us down all over. I could see, across the hall, that the horses were similarly being sponged down. Then he dried us, and brushed and combed our hair. He touched up our make-up with kohl, henna and paint.

He stood back and looked carefully at each of us. He nodded to himself.

We were ready. Ready to be auctioned!

Chapter 18

THE AUCTION RING

I heard the buzz of voices building up from behind the small door.

Several Arab horses were being led to the holding pen in front of it. A bell rang and the first horse was led prancing through the door. I heard a man's loud voice and cries from other men, then what might have been the tap of a gavel, and the next horse was led in.

After an hour they started on the women, taking the field slaves first. I heard a great cry as Hassan Ali's first bald headed woman was led through the door. It was clearly a clever move to have shaved their heads.

Then came the milk slaves, greeted by a roar. Evidently these unfortunate women were in great demand. Hassan Ali certainly knew what he was doing.

Meanwhile our overseer had unlocked us from our platforms and we now stood in a line inside the holding pen by the door.

I was trembling with nervousness. I was in such a state that if my belly had not been empty I might well have disgraced myself. The dangerous moments were obviously whilst a girl was being intimately examined on the platform and now the first moments of her entrance into the auction ring and, I supposed, the final moments of her sale. If a girl disgraced herself then, her sale would be ruined.

Bashir Aga was standing where he could see the auction ring. I saw him push Isabella through the door: she made her much practised entrance as if showing off a dress. I heard a male roar of appreciation. Then the eunuch closed it firmly behind her.

The eunuch bent down and adjusted the frilly bow round my neck and my silly little skirt. I longed for something to cover my breasts and my bare intimacies. For a moment I covered them with my hands. The Negro raised his cane. Hastily I raised my hands again and put them behind my back in the position I'd been taught for my entrance. I knew that with my manacled hands behind my back my slightly drooping breasts would be raised and my painted beauty lips, prettily outlined with henna and kohl, made more prominent.

There was a roar of voices and the tap of a gavel. It did not take long to sell a woman in Marsa!

"Start running!" ordered the black eunuch.

I began to run on the spot, raising my knee up to the level of my waist. He flung open the door and pushed me through.

I found that I was running round a small pit, ten yards across. Round the pit were high metal bars curved down at the top with a sharp point, to prevent any animal, or human, from trying to jump out. On one side was a raised rostrum for the auctioneer and his staff. All round the pit were rows of seats rising up steeply, packed with men. In the middle of the pit was a Negro with a whip. He cracked it behind me and with a gasp I went on running. Round and round. There was a roar from the crowd as I stumbled momentarily before continuing prancing round, my breasts bouncing, my knees raised.

I heard the voice of the auctioneer calling out in Arabic. I suppose he was giving my Lot Number, my age, the fact that I was a certified virgin, the weight of my breasts and my official country of origin, Italy. There were several shouts from the buyers. I heard the auctioneer saying the name of Hassan Ali. Doubtless he was saying that I was a trained brothel slave, trained by the House of Hassan Ali, which clearly counted for a lot. As I ran round, I could feel sawdust on the stone floor, mixed with the wastes of the horses which had been sold before they started on the women. The auctioneer gave an order. The Negro with the whip held it in front of me to make me stop. I stood panting, facing the men, my naked breasts rising and falling.

The bids were coming in from men in the first couple of rows. Evidently they were the interested brothel owners and the others merely spectators. I saw the huge fat Moor who had first examined me so callously raise his hand.

He was hideous. I looked round hoping to see the Bey. He wasn't there! I felt sick with disappointment.

"Kneel up! Hands over head like dancing. Now sway."

The long two months of training was paying off. I felt that I was moving and swaying beautifully and gracefully like a dancer.

"Stand up! Position for dancing, legs apart. Bend knees. Belly dance!"

There was another roar of approval.

"Turn round! Dance! Dance!"

I knew that the Moors liked a woman's bottom. I wriggled and swayed just as I had been taught.

Only two men were now bidding. To my horror I saw that one was the gross hideous Moor. He cried out as if raising his bid considerably. There was a sudden silence. I stood quite still, still displaying myself shamelessly. There was the tap of a gavel. I had been sold to the Moor!

A door was opened in the side of the pit. The Negro with the whip motioned with it for me to run through it, then I was suddenly seized. I was now in a room full of small cages containing women. Before I could protest, I was hustled into one. It was tiny. I was held crouching, doubled up, as the cage was lifted up by two burly Negroes and placed on top of another cage. I saw that the other one contained a frightened looking Isabella. Both cages had been put to one side. Had we both been bought by the same hideous Moor? A canvas hood was dropped over the barred side of the front of the cage. I could now see nothing, but I could hear the sound of the sale continuing and periodically the door was opened as another woman was pushed through.

Suddenly the canvas of my cage was lifted up and a Negro slid aside the bars of my cage. He had a powerful pair of metal wire cutters in his hands as he reached into the cage and pulled me forward by my collar. With a sudden snip he cut off the disc that proclaimed I was the property of Hassan Ali and replaced it with another. He squeezed the new disc tight onto my collar before closing and locking the bars of my cage. He pulled down the canvas cover and once again I was in darkness.

I felt the cage being lifted up, and heard new voices. Vaguely I realized the cage was being strapped on to the side of some animal. I felt the cage sway as the animal moved off. Greatly daring, I whispered, "Isabella?"

"That black who bought us," I asked anxiously. Who is he?"

"I think he owns a fonduk. A sort of an expensive brothel."

Not daring to say more, I crouched in silence in my tiny cage. I felt we were climbing up a slope. The cage seemed to sway. There were voices all round us - it was clearly a busy place, with all the usual smells and noises of an eastern town.

At last we stopped. A gate was opened. A eunuch's voice spoke in Lingua Franca:

"Two new girls for the Silver Cage."

PART FOUR
BROTHEL SLAVE

Chapter 19

THE 'SILVER CAGE'

Isabella and I were kneeling at the feet of the gross and hideous Hamid Hussein, the owner of the 'Silver Cage' and now of us both. As was normal in Marsa, the 'Silver Cage' combined the functions of both a cabaret and a brothel. Hamid Hussein held the leads to our collars in one hand and the stem of a Turkish water pipe in the other.

It was the morning after he had purchased us at the auction. He had just tried us out as singers and belly dancers. Naked, except for our collars and manacles, we had displayed our repertoire - singing and dancing in the Arab way, standing on the little stage that was raised above the now empty cabaret, our leads held throughout by a little black boy carrying a dog whip.

His huge frame resting on the sofa from which he would later supervise the evening's activities and chatter to his friends and clients, Hamid Hussein had watched us rehearse and perform, his Arab musicians squatting with their instruments by the side of the stage.

Whilst one of us had performed, wriggling and swaying nervously and sinuously in front of him, and singing like little girls in the Moorish style, the other had to please him, crawling up under his voluminous robes and trying desperately to excite him with tongue and fingers.

He had made no comment on our performances, either on the stage or under his robes. Now he motioned his principal assistants to come over to him: Nur, the Moorish dancing mistress, a woman of about forty with a still voluptuous figure; Mafa, the Negro eunuch who had the title of the Master of the Cage; and Freeka, the big young Negress who was Mistress of the Alcoves.

To one side of him was a large prominent cage, some six foot high with bars all round and over the top. The bars appeared to be of solid silver and obviously worth a fortune. It was this that gave the luxury establishment its name. The cage jutted into the room so that its contents could be seen easily by men sitting at the various divans and low Moorish-style brass tables.

We had been told by Mafa that, in the evening and at night when the cabaret was open, the twenty or so white whores had to stand in the cage, wearing their transparent silken caftans. These had the Silver cage emblem embroidered on the left breast and the girl's brothel number embroidered in red on the right breast. Each girl's collar lead was fastened tightly to one of the bars of the cage, ensuring that she was well displayed.

I had been told that my brothel number was nine and Isabella's was fifteen. We had been given the numbers of the two girls whom we had apparently replaced. They had attracted the attention of the black Ambassador from the Negro Kingdom of Agades, far to the south across the Sahara Desert. Marsa apparently maintained a close trading relationship with this Kingdom and the Ambassador had bought the two girls from Hamid Hussein. Now, apparently, he would be taking the two pretty European girls back with him as a present to his master, M'gar, the King of Agades.

Mafa had explained to us that the clientele of the cabaret would sit on the low divans, or piles of cushions, that surrounded the little stage, drinking Turkish coffee or sherbets, smoking kef and eating a bewildering variety of sweetmeats and tasty dishes. These would all be served by white page boys, whom I had seen wearing the long swirling skirts of a dancing boy, under which they were naked. They also wore the distinctive tall white pointed caps that signified a eunuch. Their budding little breasts were half hidden by embroidered waistcoats which also the emblem of the Silver cage embroidered on the left side, and on the right, like us, an Arabic numeral. However their numbers were blue to distinguish them from ours, which were red.

Mafa explained that clients would walk around the cage and choose one or more girls to attend on him and his friends, whilst they ate and drank. He would simply tell Mafa, as the Master of the Cage, the brothel numbers of the girls he wanted. The Negro would then unlock the cage and lead us over to the client. It was, we already knew, a strict rule that whilst the page boys were free to come and go, fetching food and drink from the kitchens, no girl was ever let off her leash.

We had been told that we must never go anywhere, at any time, unless we were being led by Hamid Hussein or Mafa themselves, by Nur or Freeka, by a client or, more normally, by one of the half dozen little black boys that Mafa had to help him control the brothel girls. These little black boys, each armed with a dog whip which they clearly enjoyed using, would hold our leads and stand over us while we washed, while we dressed, while we ate our dull slave porridge (the boys, of course, were allowed delicious food and plenty of sweets), whilst we passed water or relieved ourselves, and even whilst we danced on the little stage.

Once our leads had been given to the client we were to kneel at his feet, smiling happily up at him, stroking and kissing his feet, offering him glasses of sherbet or tiny cups of coffee or sweet mint tea, or plates of Eastern sweetmeats, saturated in butter, pastries filled with almond paste, delicious pieces of roasted pigeon, and other delicacies. It was our task to put them into his mouth. We would be hoping, of course, that the client might put a sweet or delicacy into our mouths for a second or two, but we must never beg or suggest it. Moreover we were never to actually swallow the sweet or delicacy, but had to put it carefully back on the dish remembering that Mafa and his little black boys would be watching to see that we did so.

We were only allowed to eat once a day, early in the morning, and had to empty ourselves in the evening before the clients arrived so that our bodies would be pure and clean for their use. We were not allowed to talk without permission and we were not to annoy the clients by interrupting their talk with requests, such as: "Master, may a slave speak?" We were to be seen and felt, but not heard! We were just animals.

Indeed, we were to allow our clients to fondle and stroke our heads and bodies, just as if we were animals. Even though our caftans were transparent, they were split up the sides to the hip, and down from the neck to the waist in the front and back. We were told that these slits were to give our clients provocative little glimpses of our breasts and intimacies and give them full access to them. Whilst a girl, or boy, was dancing erotically on the stage, we were to put our heads under the client's robes and please him just as we now had to do to our Master, Hamid Hussein.

When it was our turn to get ready to dance, Mafa or one of his little black slave boys would bring out another girl from the cage on a lead to take our place, and ask permission of the client to lead us away and hand us over to Nur, the dancing mistress. She would then dress us in our costume, rehearse us briefly and make us sing a few notes to clear our voices, whilst all the time a little black boy would still be holding our lead.

128

If the client wished to withdraw to one of the curtained alcoves with one or more of the girls, or perhaps with a page boy as well, either while the need was on him, or for the night, then he would summon Freeka, the Negro Mistress of the Alcoves, and make the necessary arrangements. He would also tell Freeka how he wanted us to be dressed and chained in the alcove, and she would then lead us off to be prepared for him.

All this had been told to us quite clearly and explicitly. I had found it deeply shocking and humiliating, but I had to recognize that it was just what we had been trained and disciplined to do in Hassan Ali's establishment. At least the Bey would hardly be likely to come to this sort of establishment and see my utter degradation.

Finally, we had been shown the Marking Board. This listed the brothel numbers of all the girls down one side and on the other the number of marks each had earned during the present week. One mark was given for each time a girl was chosen from the cage to attend on a client, and two marks every time she was sent to await him in an alcove.

Every Friday morning, after Prayers in the mosques, the three top girls were rewarded. Three sweets were given to the top girl, two to the second and one to the third. Deprived as we were of anything sweet, these were a much longed for award - and a powerful incentive to perform well. At the same time however, the six girls who were bottom of the list were punished: twelve strokes for the bottom girl, ten for the girl one from bottom, eight for the next one and so on.

We were shown the instrument that would be used for these punishments - a thick leather oval shaped paddle, mounted on a long flexible handle. Its advantage over the cane or whip, we were told, was that when applied to a girl's backside it left no unsightly weal.

These punishments were administered by Mafa on the stage of the cabaret, the girls being summoned from the cage one by one and led tearfully and apprehensively by one of the little Negro boys up to the stage. Each punishment was a long drawn out affair with much kissing of the paddle, invocations to Allah, and adjustments to the girl's position between each stroke. When each punishment was over, the now sobbing girl, holding her bottom like a little child that has been chastised, was put back into the cage.

The administration of these punishments was a very popular spectacle. After watching any public executions and punishments on the Square outside the principal mosque of Marsa, many of the wealthier men of the town would flock into the 'Silver Cage' to see the girls being given the paddle. It was good for trade since many men, aroused by the spectacle, would immediately want to choose a girl from the cage to take to an alcove to slake their lust - often choosing one of those whom they had just watched squirming and crying on the stage. Thus the girls who were bottom of the list in one week were often given a good start for the next one.

Hamid Hussein had devised a further devilishly clever way of ensuring the enthusiastic collaboration of all his girls, and thus of boosting his profits. After the first three days of each week, the list was taken down and kept in secret by Mafa. With even the least popular girls being summoned from the cage perhaps several times in an evening, the difference in marks was not all that great, and it was soon impossible for an individual girl to know for certain just how she was doing. She just had to go on trying harder and harder to catch the eyes of clients and then to please them.

Even when the regular Friday beatings began, we wretched girls in the cage would still not know which of us were going to be beaten until our numbers were called out. To heighten the drama further, Mafa would start with the girl who had earned only two strokes and then work up, two strokes at a time, until he ended up with the girl who was going to get twelve - by which time half of us were almost hysterical with fear and trepidation, thus further arousing the audience. The effect of this long drawn out suspense can be imagined, especially as Mafa would never give us even a hint as to whether or not we were likely to be in the bottom six of the list.

Naturally we were always very worried lest Mafa had not recorded all our marks. Similarly, the temptation to cheat by claiming more assignments than we had achieved was very strong. However Mafa, as Master of the Cage, kept an accurate record and so did Freeka, as Mistress of the Alcoves. False claims were punished, as were any bad reports on our performance by clients, with ten marks being deducted from our score - and almost certain sentence to a beating at the end of the week.

"You girls," Freeka had explained with a grim smile, "who are near bottom of list in middle of week, will do anything to attract a man and please him, whilst girls well up list will struggle desperately to keep their place. You soon understand!"

I could believe it. I looked at the paddle. It was terrifying.

"I see that Hassan Ali's training system has not lost its touch," said the corpulent Hamid Hussein as we knelt at his feet. He turned to his assistants.

"We have two quite good girls here." He pointed at Isabella. "This one, Number 15, will dance tonight. See to it Nur! I will also try her out myself this afternoon after my lunch."

I heard poor Isabella gasp. He was a revolting looking man, and so huge!

"And now, what will we do with our little virgin? I think I will have her dance the Virgin Dance in three nights. I will see that it is published round the town. Meanwhile, she is not to be seen by the clients. I want

131

her to be a surprise, so that, Allah willing, we have a big crowd. You, Nur, please see that she practises her dancing. It must be perfect. You, Mafa, will be responsible for selling the tickets. We will draw one First Ticket, one Boy's Type Ticket and ten Follow-Up ones."

I was listening with a mixture of horror and puzzlement. What was a Virgin Dance? Why did it have to be published around the town?

Hamid Hussein's gross body moved uneasily on the sofa. He leant down ponderously and patted my head.

"Yes, my dear, I think you are going to do very well here for me," he said. "Now pay attention both of you. Look up at me! Listen carefully! You have already been told about most of the house rules. Now there is another point I want you both to remember at all times. You are never to touch any of the money a client may pay for your services. You are not even allowed to possess a purse. Money is not your business. Freeka, here, is responsible for negotiating for your services with a client. If I ever find you with any money in your possession, even if it is only just to buy a few sweets, you will be punished for theft. Twenty four strokes of the whip for the first offence, and what Number Nine is the punishment in Marsa for a second theft?"

"Our right hand is struck off, Master," I said terrified, almost in a trance as I remembered the Warning we had been given.

The voice of my Master brought me back to the present.

"There is just one little preliminary left. You will both now undergo a little operation."

I gave a gasp of horror. I heard Isabella whimper.

"No, you are not going to be circumcised, or not yet, anyway. It is just nipple rings - for the moment!"

Chapter 20

THE RAFFLE

It was now three days since my arrival at the 'Silver Cage'. I stood trembling behind the long bead curtain beyond which was the little stage on which I was soon to perform my Virgin's Dance.

During my training Mafa had taken me out of the cage and carefully washed me all over like a little girl. I was to learn that he did this to each girl every day. He had a little book in which he recorded all the intimate details of each girl, as well as her weight and measurements, including those of a most private nature. I felt so humiliated answering his probing questions as he made his notes and took his measurements. Then he had given me my silken lace transparent kaftans. They were lovely, but I was told I was only to wear them when the cabaret was open and when I was in the silver cage or attending on a client. The rest of the time I was to wear a simple short house tunic. In my own cage, of course, I was naked.

Nur, the dancing mistress, was finishing dressing me for my dance. She strapped rows of little bells to my wrists and ankles, and hung two larger and deeper toned bells from my nipples. I could feel their weight - they rang at the slightest quiver. Long strips of white silk ribbon hung down to my ankles, fastened by little clips to a silken cord round my shoulders. Thus, until I moved I was completely hidden by the ribbons, but the slightest movement resulted in my nipples thighs and bottom appearing through the ribbons in an erotic and entrancing way.

Underneath the ribbons, I was naked except for a loose belt of bright metal coins that hung on my hips drawing attention to my painted beauty lips. I so dreaded having to appear like this in front of men.

I could hear Mafa calling out in Arabic and occasionally in Lingua Franca. I saw that the cabaret was packed. I knew that they had come to see me. I wondered why, since I was only an inexperienced beginner.

"Buy your ticket at half price now, Masters!" I heard Mafa call as he walked round between the crowded sofas and piles of cushions. "Buy unseen now. Tickets will be double the price as soon as she is brought in, and double again when she dances."

Freeka held me tightly by two leads. I knew that when I danced two little Negro boys, standing on either side of me, would each hold one of the leads fastened to my gleaming collar to give a more erotic effect. I had had to rehearse with them.

There were cries in Arabic and Lingua Franca from the audience. They were getting impatient. I understood one of the cries.

"Bring on the virgin! Bring on the virgin!"

I shuddered again. Freeka held my leads very tight now.

Hamid Hussein stood beside me. The cries grew louder. He nodded to Freeka. She handed the leads to the two little Negro boys each wearing satin suits and turbans with a tall feather fastened in the front.

"Hands up!" hissed Nur. Biting my lips, I put my chained wrists above my head, the backs of the palms touching, just as I had so often practised. Hamid Hussein parted the bead curtain and the two Negro boys stepped out onto the small stage.

"Last chance to buy unseen!" came the voice of Mafa. "Two tickets Master? And ten for you Master?"

There was a pause. The cabaret grew quiet. Suddenly I felt sharp tugs from the leads. I was being drawn onto the stage. I looked round wildly. No escape. I stepped through the beaded curtain.

There was a moment's silence, and then the roar of men's voices.

I stood quite still, just as Nur had rehearsed me.

I heard men's voices shouting at Mafa to buy tickets.

"Three over here! I want six! Bring me four!"

The stage was now brightly lit, leaving the rest of the cabaret half in the dark except for the lamps that lit up the silver cage and its beautiful occupants.

The voices ceased. The musicians began to play. Slowly I let my hands drop down, stroking my breasts, my belly and my thighs, brushing aside the long white ribbons. Then I slowly raised my hands again above my head and slowly began to sway in a sensuous dance. I was an innocent little girl, a nervous little fawn, a pretty little thing, a virgin! As I swayed to the haunting music my hands now mimed playing with a doll, then waving happily as if to friends, and then charmingly picking bunches if flowers. I was carried away by my dancing. I really was a little girl again.

The cabaret was strangely quiet but I could hear occasional cries of:

"I'll take ten! And so will I!"

Then suddenly the tempo of the music changed. It became faster and more urgent. The drum beats mirrored a man's heavy footsteps. Now I began to act. Desperately, as I had rehearsed, I looked round. I was scared. I was frightened. I tried to run away, but the leads held me tight. I put my hands over my eyes. I pressed my knees close together.

One of the little Negro boys reached up and unclipped one of the long ribbons that ran down my back. It fluttered to the floor. I gestured as if trying to pick it up. Another ribbon fluttered down. I writhed despairingly. Now the ribbons hanging down my front also began to fall. I clutched my breasts anxiously. I writhed to the music. One by one the ribbons were falling. There were cries from the audience, cries of appreciation, and more cries to buy more of those strange tickets.

As the last ribbons slipped to the floor I hid my intimacies with cupped hands in the natural gesture of a little girl, of a virgin. Again I looked around desperately for somewhere to run. The Negro boys held the leads tight, just as we had rehearsed.

The music became muted, leaving the drum beat dominant. With each beat I stepped back with a jolt. My hands were now outstretched in front of me, as I slowly stepped backwards round the little stage, as if trying to push someone away. I knew that my body was now naked to the men's gaze, just like the girl I was miming. I felt my cheeks, my neck and my breast beginning to blush. There was another roar of appreciation.

Again a sharp change in the music. I raised my hands above my head, backs of palms touching again, as if they were held in a man's hands. I parted my legs as if his other hand was touching me there. My knees were bent. I began to writhe and shake as if trying to wriggle out of his grasp. But I was tightly held. Slowly, very slowly, I began to respond to his touch my belly rolling and my knees alternatively closing tightly and then opening again. My breasts were heaving, the two deep toned bells ringing stridently. My hands still were held above my head, I could not help myself reacting ever more wildly to his touch. I writhed my hips as if trying to shake off his hand, but in vain. My belly was now wriggling strangely in the erotic movement of the belly dance, as I mimed the increasing arousal of a touched girl.

Then I was no longer miming. I was really aroused! I felt moist and hot. There was another roar of appreciation.

They could see the wetness of my beauty lips, painted and framed by the jingling line of metal coins and the infibulation rings.

I recognized a particular double drum beat. I dropped to my knees as if pushed down by a strong man. I continued to writhe, my belly wriggling. I looked up at him, begging him to spare me. I clasped my hands behind my neck as if he had fastened them to my collar. Now he was playing with me with two hands. I turned my head wildly from side to side, my tongue darting in and out as I fought off the approaching ecstasy. My shoulders heaved and wriggled as I tried to throw off the hand now stroking my breasts. My belly writhed in response to the hand between my legs.

Gracefully I slid to the floor as if pushed down by my strong attacker, my parted legs to the audience. I continued to belly dance. I raised myself to him. It was as if I was raising myself to the audience, offering myself to them. Again there was a roar. I writhed madly and then as the music suddenly stopped, flung myself outstretched on the floor, conquered and possessed.

Again there was a sudden silence and the a continuous roar from the audience.

I felt sharp tugs on my collar. Obediently I knelt up and then put my head to the floor, the palms of my hands flat on the floor, my hair flung forward over my head in the gesture of abject servility that I had been taught.

I heard the calls for tickets multiply. I knelt there. I had been warned that something would now happen but I did not know what.

It was the voice of a man. An angry voice, a protesting voice. He was shouting in Arabic and then repeating himself in Lingua Franca.

"That's no virgin! No virgin could dance like that! Cheat! Fraud! I want my money back!"

The little black boys holding my leads, kept me quite still. I did not even dare look up as the uproar continued.

There were heavy footsteps onto the boards of the stage. Out of the corner of my eye I saw Hamid Hussein coming to the front of the platform. As the shouts increased, he held up his hand for silence. Slowly the shouts died down. When he spoke in Lingua Franca I understood the gist of what he was saying.

"My friends! Do you not believe me? ... You say she can't be a virgin ... on my honour ... one of you will soon know ... you want to know now? Very well. Is there a physician present? Or a barber? ... Sir, this is a certificate attesting to her virginity. Will you come and check her for yourself and countersign the certificate? Come up to the platform, Sir."

There were cries of approval. I saw a man in the customary blue robes of a physician pushing his way towards the platform.

"Turn round Number Nine!" ordered Hamid Hussein. I hesitated, for I was still kneeling on all fours. The Negro boys pulled my leads. Blushing once again, I turned round. Now I was facing away from the audience.

"Put your head down! Legs wide apart! Back straight!"

I felt his foot on my neck. I was quite helpless as the physician knelt down behind me.

Suddenly I gave a jerk. There was a roar from the crowd.

Slowly and gently he checked the existence of my virginity. He did it twice, as if not sure. Finally he withdrew his fingers. He stood up. He turned to the audience.

"It is true! She is a virgin!"

There was another great roar of appreciation.

The physician countersigned the certificate. It was read out by Hamid Hussein. There were more cries of appreciation. I still knelt there, my beauty lips shamefully on display.

"There are still a few tickets left," said Hamid Hussein in a casual voice. Immediately the room was filled with cries.

"I'll take another two! ... Four here! ... I want another ten! ... Let me have twenty!"

The renewed selling went on for several minutes. I still knelt proffering myself. This was all something in which I had not been rehearsed - perhaps deliberately so as to make it seem more natural. I did not know what to do any more than I knew what the tickets were for. I remembered the paddle I had seen. I kept quite still.

"Look up, Masters, look up at what you may be lucky to be enjoying in a few minutes time."

It was the voice of Mafa. There was another spate of selling more tickets.

Then I heard cries of: "The Draw! ... The Draw!"

Freeka slipped back on to the platform. She held something in her strong hands. It looked like a hood, it was a hood! Quickly she strapped it over my head and strapped it shut but it was only half a hood. It came down to my upper lips only. I could see nothing, but my mouth was uncovered.

I was jerked to my feet by the leads. I was turned round. I realized that I now stood naked facing the audience. Shyly I covered myself with my chained hands.

"The Draw! The Draw!"

The shouts increased.

"Put out your right hand," ordered Hamid Hussein. I reached out. I felt the top of a large bowl.

"Draw a ticket!"

I did so. He took it and shouted out a number, then I heard a man's shriek of triumph and more excited voices.

"Now draw out the second ticket, the one as for a boy!" came the order. I did not understand what was happening. Again, I drew a ticket. Again I heard Hamid Hussein

139

shout out a number. Again I heard a man's shriek of triumph.

"Now draw out ten more!" The horror of what was to come was dawning on me. Trembling, I drew out ten more tickets. Each was announced and greeted with a shriek of delight, though perhaps not quite so ecstatically as the first two.

"Take her, Freeka, and chain her in the Royal Cubicle."

Quite unable to see anything, I was led away, stumbling. I understood it all now. I heard the voice of Hamid Hussein.

"Sirs, if you have been unlucky, don't despair! Look at the pretty girls that still await you in the cage!"

Chapter 21

THE WINNERS GET THEIR PRIZE

Freeka took me into one of the alcoves. I heard her draw the curtains. She removed the belt of metal coins that had been wound round my waist and the bells from my ankles, wrists and nipples. She sponged my sweating body down my back, over my breasts and then down over my beauty lips, and then tapped me with her little dog whip.

"Down!"

I lay down on my back. I found that I was lying on a large soft mattress. It was the first time that I had been allowed to lie on a mattress since my capture - up to now I'd had to make do with a thin blanket or a piece of carpet or straw - and always on the hard floor.

She raised my chained wrists above my head and fastened the chain to the wall. I felt her take hold of my left ankle and fasten a manacle round it. Then she did the same with the other ankle. My feet were now held wide apart and raised about a foot above the bed, held it seemed by chains hanging down from the ceiling. My knees were slightly bent.

I felt her doing something to me. Inserting something.

"Now you won't conceive!" said Freeka.

I had been hooded when I drew the winning number, and I was still hooded - I would never know who my ravisher was.

My ravisher!

He was coming.

I heard the curtains part again. I heard a man's footsteps. I heard Freeka leave, drawing the curtains again. I was alone with a man who was going to take my virginity. Chained and helpless, I heard him slip out of his robes.

I started to sob, but I knew he would not relent. This was what I had been trained for by the House of Hassan Ali. This was what I had been bought for - to earn money for my Master by the sale of my body, and initially by the sale of my virginity.

The man laughed at my cries. Suddenly I felt his hand on my leg. It travelled up slowly, caressingly. Another hand was on my breast. I could not help myself from responding, responding increasingly wildly as he played with my chained and wriggling body.

He kissed my leg. He kissed my breasts. He kissed my belly. I could not stop myself from crying out with pleasure. The minutes seemed hours.

"Oh! Oh!"

Then to my undying shame I heard myself crying out: "Don't stop! Don't stop!"

He gripped my hair tightly. He pulled my face up to his bearded chin. I was helpless, deliciously helpless. I was a chained slave, an eager chained slave. Just as I had been taught, I reached up with my tongue and humbly licked his chin, like a little dog in a gesture of complete submission. As a slave girl in Marsa, I knew I had no other choice. I also knew that in each cubicle hung a special slave whip for the clients use, should a girl show the slightest sign of reluctance. Terrified at the thought of being whipped, I reached up again and again, licking humbly and reverently. He knelt across me, still holding me tightly by the hair. I was now licking his manhood - still humbly and reverently. I could feel he was fully aroused, huge and hard.

It should have been Dermot ...

He took me in his arms. I was naked and aroused in a man's arms for the first time. And hooded so that I could not see him. He held me very tightly, and then with a sudden thrust penetrated me. In a minute I was no longer a virgin. He was deep inside me. I could feel the blood on my thighs. I screamed and screamed and heard nothing but laughter from beyond the curtain.

He held me quite still, and ran one hand down my body. Again I could not help myself from responding. For several minutes he continued, bringing me to a peak of excitement, before I felt him erupt, inundating me. I was momentarily grateful for Freeka's attentions, for otherwise surely I would have been impregnated. How could my body have resisted such a flood? But I knew that breeding from a slave was a matter for the Master to decide and control. In Europe a woman in an interesting condition was eschewed by men, but I knew that in the Orient, on the contrary, men found an increased delight from a woman in such a state. Several of the prettiest girls in the 'Silver Cage' had been deliberately allowed to become pregnant. They were amongst the most sought after girls in the cage and the most appreciated when forced to dance naked on the stage. I knew it was only a question of time before Hamid Hussein decided that I too would earn him a greater dividend on his investment in me if I too had a gently swelling belly ...

I felt the man withdraw, leaving me unfulfilled.

Once again, ashamed, I heard myself begging: "Don't go! Please don't go!"

Suddenly my face was slapped hard, twice, I could taste blood in my mouth. I gasped with surprise. Then I remembered that it was presumptuous for a mere slave to beg in such a way.

Frightened of another blow, I lisped as I had been taught to do, "This little slave hopes that her Master enjoyed her."

Enjoyed me, I thought bitterly, he had taken my virginity! Anxiously trying to hide my secret thoughts I raised myself to him, offering myself again to him for his pleasure.

I heard the curtains part. I heard Freeka come into the alcove again. I was unfastened, and then chained down on my knees, my head to the ground, my legs wide apart.

I felt a man's hands behind me, a different man! He gripped me firmly as I writhed in protest in my chains. This was awful! Suddenly I remembered about the Boy's Type Ticket and realized what was coming ...

He took a long time - it seemed an age of torment before I heard the curtains being parted. Again Freeka unfastened me. At least my sufferings were now over. But she chained me again on my back in the same position as I had been when I lost my virginity. I felt another man come down onto me. The first of the ten 'Follow-Up' tickets ...

Just the first ...

Sullenly, in a gesture of despair and protest, I lay quite still as I felt him penetrate me. Let this awful man do his worst, I thought. He would get no pleasure from me! Suddenly I felt a line of fire across the sole of one of my feet.

"Dance, slave, dance!" came the voice of Freeka and she again brought her dog whip down across my foot. It was almost as painful as Bastinado! I realized that Freeka was now in the cubicle standing over me, making sure that I performed properly. I knew from my lessons at the House of Hassan Ali what she meant. Belly dancing is intended not merely as a spectacle to arouse and excite men, but also in more intimate moments as a way of giving exquisite pleasure of a very explicit nature.

I felt the man move inside me.

"Dance, slave, dance!" came the order again.

Urgently and desperately, fearing the dog whip, I began to dance. I knew that the rotations of my hips and the thrust and furious wriggling of my belly were giving intense pleasure to this hateful unknown man, a man who had won third place in the raffle. Slowly I found that I too I was being aroused again. Horrified, I stopped for a moment.

"Go on!" came the voice of the Negress, this time more quietly. She again tapped the sole of my foot with her dog whip. "Not fight it!"

I knew what she meant. I knew only too well what she meant. I was a slut, a slut becoming aroused by belly dancing on my back, held in the arms of an unknown man who had deeply penetrated me. I was a slut alright. But oh how I enjoyed being a slut! These devilish Moors had driven away the last vestige of the prudish and innocent young Irish woman. I was enjoying being chained and held helpless. I was enjoying being an Arab brothel slave. I heard myself shrieking out my pleasure, as I danced under the weight of an unknown Moor.

Several hours later I lay chained in the alcove, but now on my belly again. I could not clearly differentiate between the various unseen men who had used me. One had told Freeka to unfasten my ankles and had fastened the chain linking my wrists to another chain hanging from the ceiling. I had to kneel across him, with my hands raised above my head. I had to belly dance again as he enjoyed me as I knelt over him. The last man had had me chained down like the second man on all fours. It was almost as painful as the first time.

The cabaret was now silent. The musicians had departed. The clients had left. The girls had been taken out of the cage and put into their sleeping cage. Only a few, hired for the night, were still in the various alcoves.

I was alone with my thoughts. I was no longer a virgin. I was a slut. I had almost enjoyed my rape. I had enjoyed being taken by the other men. I enjoyed being a slave at the mercy of men. I was deeply ashamed. How could I ever look an Irishman in the face again?

I heard the curtain part again, then hands unfastening my shackles. I was free! I felt my hood being drawn off. It was Hamid Hussein himself. He was naked, his huge belly gross and repulsive. In his hand he held a little dog whip. I was terrified as he held me by my hair so that my face was only inches from his gross manhood.

"You did well Number Nine, very well."

With his other hand he stroked my cheeks like a man fondling a favourite pet dog.

"But now, first of all, you will please me, you little Christian Dog! And you will do so of your own free will, free to crawl and not chained. Look at the wall!" He pointed to the paddle hanging there. "It will remain there, whilst you show me that you are eager to please. I shall reach for it, however, at the first sign of any hesitation. I shall now lie back here, and you will work! And tomorrow you will be sore and will be allowed to rest for the whole day. Then it will be the silver cage for you. And remember that today is only the start of the week. A Virgin Dance does not count for marks."

It wasn't fair! Why shouldn't the men who had taken me that night count? Why should I have only five days to earn sufficient marks to keep out of the bottom six, when all the other girls would have had seven? It wasn't fair! But I did not dare protest - not with the paddle hanging on the wall within the reach of Hamid Hussein. Exhausted by my ordeal, I had to drive myself to kneel down humbly at his side by his fat odious stomach. He was my owner! I bent my head and began to lick as if my life depended on it.

Chapter 22

THE FRIDAY BEATINGS

I had now been a pleasure slave in the 'Silver Cage' for three months, three months of being a prize whore, three months of earning large sums for my Master, three months of serving Moorish men, and three months of being chained day and night.

Hamid Hussein had made Isabella and I dance together, and we had proved to be a popular duo for his brothel. The idea of seeing us belly dance, half naked, side by side, had brought in many rich clients, as had the embarrassing little intimate exhibitions that we had been forced to put on together on the stage under the direction of Freeka. The sight of two virtually naked white women forced to embrace each other by fear of the dog whip of a burly young Negress, whilst their collar leads were held by smartly dressed young Negro boys, was clearly a sight that wealthy Moors would pay to watch.

We had learned to hate and fear Freeka as much as we had both hated and feared the huge brutal eunuch Bashir Aga in the House of Hassan Ali. By contrast Mafa, the Negro eunuch here, was a much more friendly person.

He would grin when a client would point to a trembling girl chained by the neck to the bars of the cage to indicate that he wanted to have her serving him at his feet - and perhaps later in an alcove. He would be grinning when he unlocked the cage, reached into it and unfastened the girl's chain and pulled her out. He would still be grinning as he fastened a lead onto her collar and led her to the divan on which the client would be sitting.

He would be grinning again on Friday mornings when the cabaret had filled up with men come to watch the beating of the girls with the least points. He would call out the number of strokes followed by the brothel number of the girl who was going to be beaten. He would even be grinning when a few minutes later he would lead the girl, now sobbing with the pain and humiliation back to the cage filled with women all terrified that the next number he would call out might be theirs.

It was Freeka who, as Mistress of the Alcoves, had completed the instruction we had received in the House of Hassan Ali as to how two girls should behave when summoned together to the couch of a man. It was she who had insisted on the basic rule, that the client was always to feel the eager and tremulous tongue of one of us no matter what he might be doing with the other.

It was she who, a few days after our debut on the stage, had caught Isabella and I red-handed. Stimulated by the simulated passion she had made us put on for the amusement of the watching clients, and feeling lonely and ashamed, we had reached out for each other to console each other in the half darkness of the sleeping cage.

"You two sluts!" she screamed, banging her dog whip on the bars of the cage, as caught in the act we had looked up sheep-faced. "You will be reported to the Master in the morning!"

The next day we knelt naked and deeply ashamed at Hamid Hussein's feet, whilst Freeka gave an explicit description of what she had seen.

"You are here only to give pleasure to my clients and to earn money for me," he said angrily, "not to misbehave together. This time you just lose ten marks, next time I sell you as farm labourers!"

I had seen the smile on her lips, as she had led us away by our leads. Isabella and I knew that we were probably too valuable as whores to take the second threat seriously but to lose ten marks was still frightening. It was, of course, part of the devilish way of keeping us eager to please the clients.

"Choose us, Master," Isabella and I would anxiously lisp in chorus to men inspecting the women through the bars of the cage, to which we were chained by the neck as we stood naked under our transparent silken kaftans.

At the next Friday's beatings, I was terrified. Isabella and I had been fairly certain that we were not in the bottom half of the list, for another girl had had ten marks deducted for spilling coffee on a client's robes. She was called out to receive two strokes and then, much to the amusement of the watchers, sipping their mint tea or little cups of Turkish coffee, a heavily pregnant girl was called out to receive four strokes. She was horrified at the very idea and protested, as she was led up to the stage, that she was in no state to stand up to a beating. I saw the men put down their cups, and stop gossiping among themselves, as they leant forward to watch. The thrashing of a pregnant girl was always one of the highlights of the Friday beatings, and we suspected Mafa of juggling with the marks to ensure that at least one pregnant girl always featured on the list to be thrashed. He himself was an expert at inflicting pain without really harming the girl, or the progeny she was carrying for her Master.

Another girl was called out to receive six strokes.

A shy new girl, only a teenager, was then called out to receive eight strokes. Isabella and I smiled at each other and relaxed. Clearly we had escaped a beating, anyway for another week. We had both reckoned that we had been called out of the cage so often to please clients that, even allowing for the loss of marks that we had been awarded, we could not possibly be bottom or one from bottom of the list. It looked as though all was well.

Then came the high pitched voice of Mafa.

"Ten strokes." He paused. He looked around to make it appear more dramatic. I cold hear several of the clients suck their teeth in anticipation and repeat amongst themselves, "Ten strokes this time!"

"Numbers Nine and Fifteen. Ten strokes each!"

It wasn't fair! It couldn't be true!

Trembling with fear, we were led. There was another audible intake of breath from the many clients who were crowding the cabaret. The filthy swine! I realized that Hamid Hussein must have put it about that this was what was going to happen and hence the unusually big crowd.

Mafa would always position the girls differently between each stroke. One stroke with the girl facing away from the clients and touching her toes, her legs straight. The next with the girl sideways on, her knees bent. For the next stroke, the girl, or woman - for several of the brothel slaves were attractive women in their thirties or forties in order to please all tastes - was facing the audience so that they could watch her face as she first waited for, and then received, the stroke.

With twenty strokes to be divided alternatively between Isabella and I, Mafa was able to put on a very full performance indeed, making us even lie on our backs and raise our legs vertically for his paddle ...

After this shattering experience, we both resolved never to risk falling into the bottom six again. But only two weeks later, perhaps lulled into a sense of false security by our evident popularity, we were called out quite unexpectedly to receive six strokes each. And only a month later we received another six strokes after being punished with the loss of ten marks when a very young teenage boy, enjoying his first visit to a brothel, had viciously reported us, most unfairly, for not giving him full satisfaction - so that he could come and enjoy our punishment the following Friday.

It was shortly after this I tried to get a message back to Malta. Isabella and I had been chosen by a rather nice looking friendly man, who was evidently very rich. On my knees in the course of pleasing him,I exclaimed aloud: "Oh my God!"

It was, of course, strictly forbidden for a Christian to utter any reference to a God other than Allah, or indeed to speak in any language other than the Lingua Franca, but I had felt sure that I was safe since English was virtually unknown in Marsa. I was therefore startled when the man pulled me up by my hair and spoke in English with a heavy Maltese accent. "Where did you learn English?"

Frightened that he might have been offended by my unfortunate reference to God, I replied in English:

"I am British, Sir, a respectable Irish woman enslaved here by the Moors but please don't report me for using the word God, please, Sir, please!"

"Don't worry about that," he laughed. Then whilst Isabella listened, her mouth open with astonishment, but unable to understand a word, he whispered that he was a Maltese renegade. He was a gunsmith who had been ruined by the French invasion of Malta and had come to Marsa to seek his fortune. He had become a Moslem and his skills were in such demand that he had soon become rich with his own workshop turning out guns.

I whispered to him the story of my own unfortunate enslavement. I even begged him to help me.

He looked at me quietly for a long time before speaking.

"You do not know what you are asking. The British saved our island from the French, and I would like to help you, but there is nothing I can do to help you escape. It would be more than my life is worth even to try. I am sorry. You must accept the fact of your enslavement.

151

You are now a prize whore. If you are sensible you won't be disposed of for several years."

"Disposed of?" I muttered.

"Many good whores are sold as field slaves when they lose their attractiveness to clients. But only if they are strong. You are rather delicate, and so I think you're more likely to be shot."

"Shot!" I gasped in horror.

"Or drowned. Think of yourself as a favourite horse, a mare. Your master might have a filly or two from her in her old age. Then, rather than see her badly treated, he would have her put down. It is exactly the same here with white women slaves. It is something you must accept."

Before I could say anything more, shocked as I was, he muttered, "Now no more English - or I will report you for disobedience!"

He turned to Isabella and, speaking in Lingua Franca, ordered: "And you too, get down!"

Then holding us both by the hair, he lay back while we pleased him. My brain was bursting with what he had told me, but I was too frightened of being reported not to please him humbly.

That evening I whispered what he had said about being shot to Isabella.

"So what?" she replied. "Isn't it obvious? Have you seen any old white women slaves? Obviously, as your Maltese friend said, sooner or later we will be `disposed of'. Perhaps that will in any case be better than a terrible old age toiling in a chain gang under the whip. We must just live for the present. And as for him refusing to help you escape, there is no escape for white women slaves from Marsa. We must just accept the fact of our slavery."

Chapter 23

THE BANQUET

I had never been allowed out of the 'Silver Cage' - nor indeed to walk about it except on a lead. I was therefore very surprised, and excited, when one day Hamid Hussein told us that, together with a dozen other women and some dancing boys, we were being sent under the supervision of Freeka to dance, serve and entertain at a big banquet being given by a wealthy merchant.

"This is a good opportunity to show yourselves off to rich men," said Hamid Hussein as we lined up in front of him.

"You never know, if you please a man, he might buy you for his harem. You will each be given five extra marks if you behave yourselves well tonight, and earn me a lot of extra money. But I warn you," and his voice became harsh, "if I receive the slightest complaint then it won't be a mere ten marks that you lose! If necessary, we'll have a double sized beating session next Friday to recoup the money I'm expecting you girls to earn me tonight. So watch it! I should also warn you that after the last banquet one of the girls came back smiling with a little note for me. She could not, of course, read it and she thought it said what an intelligent, hard working girl she was. In fact it said that she should be given the Bastinado for insolence - for talking to a client without permission. So be careful!"

I shivered with fear. The Bastinado! I would do anything rather than face that again.

Later that day we were taken to the merchant's house, heavily veiled and shrouded in long black all enveloping robes, the hated little Negro boys holding us tightly by leashes fastened to our wrists. It was the first time I had seen Marsa properly. It was quite extraordinary to my Irish eyes, almost medieval and completely alien. The town seemed to be a complete jumble of flat-roofed buildings piled up against the hillside, and interspersed with a maze of narrow streets and cul-de-sacs. The houses were windowless at ground level and higher up were covered with arabesques and trelliswork to enable, I suppose, the owners' Moorish wives and European slave women to look out without being seen.

Each house seemed to be a secret prison for women, with no outward sign of how many, if any, were kept in it. In some places the narrow street had been roofed over to keep out the sun, making much of the town seem rather like a maze of tunnels. All of it was teeming with animals and humanity.

Camels and donkeys with large panniers strapped to their sides, and richly caparisoned mules, jostled their way past a bewildering array of human beings. The richly dressed merchants wore spotless white Moorish cloaks called haiks and jelabas, with the hoods up over their heads. There were Tuareg nomads from the Sahara, swathed in blue cloth that only left their eyes visible; Berber mountaineers with their heads swathed in turbans; and Arab peasants wrapped in cloaks of red wool. I saw plenty of Turkish Janissaries, presumably those commanded by the Bey, wearing bright red Turkish balloon trousers and long fierce moustaches. The Bey! I had almost forgotten about him!

All these men seemed immensely masculine - much more so than a similar crowd of men in Europe.

There were also naked idiots, clearly respected by the passing Moors. I also saw other heavily veiled slave girls, presumably fellow Christians, their wrist chains clinking under their all enveloping black shrouds. They were guarded by unveiled hefty looking Negresses, carrying canes, or by burly Negroes wearing the distinctive pointed caps of a eunuch.

There were also many Moorish women, free women. But they were obviously regarded as inferior by their menfolk whom they followed at a respectful distance, carrying water in quaintly shaped earthenware jars on their heads. Gaunt hungry looking dogs slunk by.

Obsequious and cringing Jews, wearing balloon black trousers and richly embroidered waistcoats, but forced by law to walk barefoot in the filth, were pushed aside by black eunuchs escorting some rich man's wife, or by prettily painted white page boys making a way for their Master. Flies clustered over the half putrid carcasses of animals, and scarcely less repulsive was the sight of so many beggars, blind, maimed and covered in sores.

The air of claustrophobia was accentuated by the variety of smells: the sweet smell of cedarwood in the Street of the Woodworkers, the sharp odours of the Spice Market, and the deplorable stench of tanneries down by a small river. A large open space was full of men listening to storytellers repeating, I was told, stories from the Arabian Nights. Others were listening to ballads of the great feats of the Arabs, songs which the crowd seemed to know by heart, often joining in the refrain. Circus actors and jugglers performed to admiring throngs. I recognized the Slave Market in which I had been exhibited and sold. I saw a stream of richly dressed men entering it. Were they going to examine the wares - just as I had been examined?

It all seemed so alien to my European eyes. No wonder Moorish men seemed to treat women with such indifference or deliberate cruelty, when indifference and cruelty was all around them. Animals staggered under huge loads - as did women. No one bothered to clean the streets. Half the buildings seemed to be crumbling despite the evident wealth of the odd glimpse into a delightful courtyard complete with fountain and Moorish arches.

It was to one such courtyard that Freeka led us. The gates were shut firmly behind us. We found ourselves in a series of high, beautifully decorated rooms with Arabic script painted on the walls, and innumerable arabesques. All around the sides of the thickly carpeted floors were sumptuous divans. Our team of pretty white dancing boys, all identically dressed in swirling green skirts and embroidered waistcoats, and wearing little red round cloth caps, was lined up along one wall facing the divans.

We were shown the little tiled floor on which we were to dance. Our own musicians had by now arrived. We took off our black shrouds and wearing only our transparent kaftans, we set about beautifying ourselves.

A Negro eunuch chamberlain came and explained that each of us was to attend on a different guest, serving him on our knees. For the guest of honour, two girls, Isabella and I, chained together as ever, would be in attendance.

We heard the noise of horses in the courtyard. The guests were arriving. The musicians began to play. A young white girl from our team began to dance and sing. The rest of us were ordered to prostrate ourselves humbly in front of the divan on which our master for the evening would shortly be sitting. We had to keep quite still and must have made a pretty sight for the arriving guests - a row of white women, naked under their brightly coloured silk kaftans, kneeling abjectly. No wonder the Moors despise Europeans!

The voices of the men came closer. Nervously I opened my legs wider and nudged Isabella to do likewise. I did not want to risk a beating for 'Lack of Respect'. I wondered what the man on whom we were to attend would be like. I was used now after serving so many men at the 'Silver Cage', at the way Moors, laughing and talking amongst themselves, would apparently completely ignore the white women kneeling at their feet - or even those kneeling under their robes. I had learnt, however, that it was dangerously deceptive to think that they did not notice all that you did.

Suddenly I heard the distinctive voice that I knew so well. The Bey! The man whom I had last seen when he had watched me being Bastinadoed, and later being displayed in the Slave Market, was actually here!

Chapter 24

SERVING THE BEY

I heard the Bey's voice come nearer and nearer. My head was to the ground. I did not dare look behind me. I was trembling with excitement. Suddenly, I realized that he was the guest of honour. Isabella and I would be attending on him!

I heard him sit down in front of me. Moving as one, Isabella and I crawled forward and started to lick the soles of his babouches just as we did those of every client who chose us at the 'Silver Cage'. It was a degrading gesture that I could never get used to, for the filth on the streets was revolting. When I had first had to do this to Hassan Ali after the long journey in the wagon, it had been a symbolic gesture. But here and at the 'Silver Cage', where the men had only just come off the streets, it was a necessary hygienic precaution to clean the soles of the mens' shoes - and to do it was a task left to a female Christian slave.

A little brass bowl of mint-scented water was placed by each divan, and the woman had to use it to rinse out her mouth.

Another bowl, long and with a narrow neck, was also placed by each divan by Moorish custom to enable a man with a girl's careful assistance to pass water without having to leave the banquet.

I saw the two bowls here at this banquet at the side of the divan on which the Bey was now seated. Humbly

Isabella and I took it in turn to wash out our mouths as we carefully licked the soles of his babouches. But what had seemed a humiliating and nauseous operation for other men, somehow seemed only right and proper for him. He was the Bey. My Bey! I began to feel that it was an honour to be allowed to lick the filth from his shoes. It was a way that a women showed her natural subservience to her Master.

As I eyed the other bowl I realized that this would be the first time I had performed such an intimate service for the man that I knew I perhaps loved and certainly feared and hated.

I wondered if he had recognized me. I wondered on the contrary if my presence at his feet had really been organized by him. Had he decided that he wished to see whether my 'arrogance and prudery' had yet been thrashed out of me? I knew now that I loved him. I could not believe he was so utterly disinterested in me as he had hitherto made out.

Each of the other guests was now joined by one of the white page boys so that he was being served by a pretty girl kneeling at his feet on one side and by a pretty boy on the other. I thought that this would be a humiliation that I would be spared for the Bey already had me serving him on my knees on the thick Oriental rugs on one side and, linked as always by our collar chain, Isabella on the other.

I thought Isabella was looking particularly beautiful that evening. Her eyes were sparkling as never before as she looked up adoringly at the handsome and elegant Irishman. I felt a sudden pang of jealousy. He was my love not hers and she knew it perfectly well. She had heard him asking Hassan Ali to have me Bastinadoed, and she had seen him return to watch it being carried out. She knew what a devastating effect a beating could have on a girl's emotions.

"He's mine!" I whispered furiously.

159

"We'll see!" Isabella whispered back, archly. I had thought she was my friend, my only friend in this awful and terrifying country. Now I hated her!

The Bey snapped his fingers. I was instantly reminded that he, like other wealthy men in the Moslem world, was used to being attended by boys as well as by women, for instantly two pretty white dancing boys joined us. The Bey kicked me aside, pushing me back alongside Isabella whilst the two heavily painted boys knelt on his other side. I saw that they were making eyes at him as, like me, they gazed up adoringly at his tall virile figure. Now I was as jealous of them as I had been of Isabella.

The rest of the evening passed as if in a dream. It was a scene of exquisite civility with these powerful and graceful men discussing the affairs of state as they relaxed in comfort on their divans and ate the most delicious morsels of roasted turkey, of chicken basted in almonds and of lamb stuffed with figs. But it was also a scene of incredible cruelty with Christian women and castrated boys kneeling half naked at their feet.

I cannot describe the banquet in detail. I was too excited by the near presence of the Bey to notice it all. I was in a seventh heaven, kneeling at the feet of the man I adored, even if there was also another beautiful woman there and two pretty boys. I remember holding up plates of delicious delicacies for him to eat and taste. I remember my jealousy of the boys growing when he tossed one of them a little something to grovel for on the floor like dogs. I remembered my jealousy of Isabella when he used her to keep warm in her mouth, but of course unchewed, some delightful other hot delicacy - a favourite form of disciplining a woman in Marsa. Several times I had to proffer my long beautifully washed and combed hair for him to wipe his hands and mouth on. It seemed a great honour.

Twice he ordered me to hold the long narrow brass bowl discretely under his robe for his use. Again I was proud he had chosen me to perform this very intimate service, and not Isabella or one of the page boys. Once again, as when licking the soles of his shoes, something that would have been humiliating and revolting to do for another man, seemed only right and proper to do for him. It made me long to really belong to him.

I was thrilled when casually he reached forward and stroked my hair whilst talking earnestly and at length with his host, sometimes in Arabic and sometimes in Lingua Franca. I could not, of course, follow properly what they were saying. They appeared to be discussing the re-establishment of effective Turkish rule over the neighbouring Barbary States. But I knew that female slaves were not supposed to listen to their Master's conversations. Our role was simply to serve and to please. I had been taught, both in the House of Hassan Ali and then in the 'Silver Cage' that the more intelligent a slave girl was, the more Moorish men enjoyed keeping her illiterate and ignorant, simply a decorative source of pleasure.

As I knelt as his feet, I felt that the Moors were right. It was enough for me that he should now occasionally deign to glance down at my pouting breasts and at my shining brass nipple rings as they pressed against my revealing lace kaftan. I felt proud every time I saw his eye momentarily switch away from his host to glance down at my nudity, or when his hands lazily strayed down to play with my breasts. I felt my loins become moist and hot. I was an aroused slave in the presence of her Master for the evening, of the Master whose slave she longed to be. Oh how I longed to be his slave! In a way that six months previously Miss Barbara Kennedy would never have believed, I was thrilled to be a chained and half naked slave at the feet of a strong man. How much, I thought, do most Irish and English women miss in life with their so-called freedom and independence.

How jealous I was when, still deep in conversation with his neighbour, he reached down and idly slipped Isabella's kaftan down over her pert little white breasts. How about mine, I had longed to scream. Mine are bigger and softer! But I knew they were not so firm as Isabella's. How I hated her!

I remember my unbelievable excitement when, in the middle of an argument, he had quietly slipped his voluminous white jelaba robe over my head. Underneath he was naked and soon erect. How eagerly and delicately I licked - as if my very life depended on it. How big and strong he was! How disappointed I was when he pushed my head down and aside and replaced me with Isabella and then with the two boys. I had to kneel helpless by his side, holding up a little tray of sweetmeats, and watching first Isabella's and then the boys' heads moving up and down under his robe as he continued his discussions. I was consumed with jealousy.

Then it was the turn of Isabella and I to dance on the tiled floor in front of the host. We both made a point of dancing to him, as the Guest of Honour, baring ourselves to him and, in mime, offering ourselves humbly to him.

Then to our great embarrassment, Freeka put us through our exhibition, just as if we were back on the stage at the 'Silver Cage'. Oh, how ashamed I was to have to embrace Isabella passionately and intimately in front of the Bey. I was so desperately ashamed. But I saw that the Bey's dark eyes were glistening as he watched us. I was shocked when I saw him snap his fingers and gesture to one of the pretty page boys to put his head down under his robes. I did not see any more, for Freeka's dog whip brought me back to what was supposed to be concentrating on - passionately embracing Isabella and passionately being embraced by her.

When the music stopped and Freeka led us back to the Bey, humbly crawling as usual on our knees, he gave an order and we had to follow him and the boys into a small beautifully appointed private room. Shocked, I saw that it was a bedroom.

He motioned Freeka to withdraw. The sheer unbelievable excitement of at last finding myself alone in a luxurious bedroom with the Bey was overwhelming - even though I was still chained to Isabella and in the company of two page boys. How many times had I imagined being alone with him. This was the next best thing.

A whip hung on the wall. He reached up for it. I trembled. But he flung it across the room.

"Fetch!" he ordered.

Isabella and I had to scurry across the room on all fours and pick up the whip in our teeth depositing it humbly at his feet. Six times he made us do this, driving the fact that we were slaves deeper and deeper into our consciousness. He was a man, a real man!

After all our training at Hassan Ali's, and our experience at the 'Silver Cage', Isabella and I were by now very good at bringing exquisite pleasure to a man. The Bey seemed pleased with our efforts. Then, as if to give our tongues a rest, he made us kneel up on either side of him, our legs apart, our heads up, our chained wrists behind our necks and our collar chain taut.

Then he began to toy with us both, whilst the page boys took over our task. Our nipple rings and our painted intimacies fascinated him. Excited as we both already were, he soon had us writhing in ecstasy.

I could feel the climax approaching fast. But it was not to be.

"Keep still, both of you! Quite still!" he ordered.

The effort of keeping still whilst being aroused by him to new peaks of excitement was overpowering and thrillingly frustrating. I longed to wriggle and to bring myself to climax into his hand, but I did not dare move a muscle. This was the most exciting man I had ever known. I adored him! I worshipped him!

Then, satisfied that we were both ready and eager for him, he suddenly stopped.

"Kneel on all fours, all four of you," he ordered. I could not help myself from raising my buttocks to him, like a bitch on heat. It was degrading, but I did not dare to refuse. I was thrilled and honoured to feel him inside me momentarily as he tried us out first in direct competition with the boys, and then, on our backs, in competition with each other as women. Isabella and I both had to show the pleasure we could give by belly dancing whilst being penetrated, something that the boys could not do and which is surely the ultimate ecstasy for a man - and the reason why for hundreds of years Eastern men have insisted on their concubine becoming adept at this difficult art.

I remember how deeply cheated I felt, and how madly jealous, when he decided to use Isabella's loins as the final source of his pleasure, leaving me and the boys to kneel behind him, driving him I hoped to greater peaks of ecstasy with our tongues. Then, as a reward, he allowed Isabella to reach a climax with him. I had to listen while she cried out in her pleasure, leaving me to watch frustrated and disappointed.

With his long lean body, his firm dominant authority and his wonderful hands he was my God. I worshipped him now more than ever. However I realized that my feelings were now fully shared by Isabella. She too was also now clearly madly in love with him, and, it seemed, he preferred her to me. Nevertheless, remembering what Hamid Hussein had said about men buying us, I longed to ask him to buy me. But remembering what Hamid Hussein had also said about insolence, I did not dare to do so.

When he left, satiated, and we were taken back to the 'Silver Cage', I felt desperately sad and disappointed. The man I loved had scarcely addressed one word to me, and had chosen my companion in preference to me. My life seemed pointless and at an end. I wept bitterly in the sleeping cage that night, whilst Isabella slept exhausted and content.

It was therefore with unbelievable surprise and excitement that Isabella heard the next day from Hamid Hussein that he had accepted an offer for us both from the Bey, whose eunuch would be coming later to pick us up.

We were both thrilled, our jealousy and rivalry forgotten. Overcome with sheer joy, we kissed each other and swore eternal love for the Bey. Somehow it seemed only natural for two girls, two slave girls, to adore equally such a commanding Master.

Hamid Hussein cut into our celebrations.

"Don't be too happy! You may soon both be wishing that you were soon enjoying a life of ease here in the 'Silver Cage'."

We laughed gayly into his face. What an idea!

We ran round the other girls accepting their congratulations and kissing them goodbye. We were overcome by happiness.

Our nipple rings were removed, and the chain linking our two collars was removed. We were no longer to be tied to each other. We would no longer have the humiliation of nipple rings. The Bey was a civilized and cultured man. He would not use such devices.

We were each packed into a tiny wooden cage, just as we had been when we were first taken to the 'Silver Cage'. The wooden cages were strapped onto mules and covered with canvas. Unable to see anything, I waited excitedly in my cage.

Then suddenly I heard the hated voice of Bashir Aga. What was he doing here? I remembered vaguely that he was going to work for the Bey on some 'craft', whatever that meant. Mystified, I heard the eunuch sign a receipt for us as if we were animals. I heard him lead the mules out into the street. Re-assured, I felt the mules starting to go downhill, presumably towards the Bey's waterside palace and his harem.

After a time I heard the lapping of water. Suddenly terrified, I remembered the stories of Turks drowning their disobedient women slaves. I remembered the story of the Maltese gunsmith of unwanted slaves being 'disposed of'. Was I going to be thrown into the harbour inside the little cage? Was this he Bey's revenge for my impertinence in Malta?

I felt the cage being unfastened. It was lifted up high. I knew that Bashir Aga was an immensely strong brute. Was he going to throw the cage into the sea? Suddenly I felt a swaying motion - I was being carried on board a boat! I heard the murmurs of voices and the clink of chains. I heard women's voices! I felt the cage being put down, and a moment later heard Isabella's cage being put down beside mine.

There were raised voices and orders, orders I did not understand, then something that sounded like the rhythmic rowing of oars. I heard the regular beat of a drum. It was varying its beat in accordance with the orders of a voice - the well known voice of the Bey. I heard the crack of a whip, followed by the cry it seemed of a woman.

Suddenly the canvas cover of my little cage was lifted up. Gripping the bars I peered through them. Then I gave a shriek, an uncontrollable shriek of horror ...

PART FIVE

Chapter 25

THE GALLEY

"No, no!" I screamed as I gripped the bars of the little cage.

It had been placed on the raised poop of a beautifully proportioned miniature galley, or galliot. It was a sort of private yacht, but not the sort I was familiar with. It was magnificently kept with its varnished woodwork and highly polished brass fittings glistening in the sun. Above the little poop was a raised curved wooden covering, like a fixed awning, evidently designed to protect whoever was on the poop from the elements, whether it was rain or sun.

The Arab coxswain, having lifted the canvas cover off my cage, went back to his position right aft at the back of the poop, by the after steering wheel. Another wheel, evidently in parallel to the after one was at the break of the poop by the steps that led down to the rowing deck. This must be in case the owner decided to both steer his vessel and to control its motive power.

Several large white covered cushions, with blue piping on the edges, were arranged around the poop. A little brass table held a Turkish hookah, or water pipe, a vase of cool-looking sherbet, and a bowl of Turkish Delight, the sight of which made my mouth water.

Up in the bows of the little galley sat a Negro boy beating out the time on a drum. By his side was a brazier on which coffee was being heated, evidently for the people sitting in the poop. A mast reached up above him, carrying the large furled Arab lanteen sail - for use, presumably, when the wind was suitable and the rowers were tired.

Behind him was a tall superstructure, raised like the poop above the low rowing deck, which seemed almost level with the sea. The raised bow was clearly intended to assist the galley in cutting through rough seas.

As with the much larger full sized galleys, this galliot was long and narrow. A long catwalk, or gangway, ran right along the rowing deck from the foot of the poop to the bow superstructure.

On either side of the catwalk were the rowing benches, ten on either side, to match the oars, each pulled by one rower, so that there were twenty rowers in all. To give the rowers better leverage, a false bulwark ran alongside each side of the vessel some three feet out from the real side of the galley. The oars rested in slots cut in this bulwark.

The rowing benches were some six feet below the level of the poop deck, and the deck on which the feet of the rowers rested was only just above the waterline. If the sea was at all rough, water would sweep along the deck, entering through small sluices cut in the galley's side - a useful way of keeping the vessel spotless. This rowing deck was of course watertight and under it, I discovered later, was a low hold - used for stowing ropes and spare oars.

Seated crosslegged on the cushions on the poop, and looking down onto the rowing deck with a satisfied smile, was the Bey. Seated alongside him were two well dressed Arabs, wearing the spotless white robes and gold embroidered keffiyah and aighal headdress that I had by now learnt to be the sign of a chieftain.

But it was not them, nor the layout of the galley, that had made me cry out in horror.

It was partly the sight of my old terrifying enemy, Bashir Aga, walking up and down the catwalk, in his hand a short black coiled whip which he was occasionally cracking menacingly. He was naked to the waist, the muscles of his black torso rippling in the sunlight, his bald head shining and his tribal tattoos and grim look all combining to make him seem even more brutal and frightening than before. This galley, I now realised, was the mysterious 'craft' for which the Bey had arranged to borrow him from Hassan Ali. He was now the galley's whip-master, in charge of the rowers, seated ten on each side, one behind the other, their wrists chained to their oars, their hair brushed back and hanging down their backs.

What had really made me scream was the realisation that the rowers were all women, naked women, beautiful women ... white slaves like myself!

The rowers were veiled, wearing a black mask that showed only their flashing eyes, outlined it seemed in black kohl to make them seem bigger. The mask was of a stiff opaque material that covered each woman's face and ended in a fringe that hung down below her chin. The mask was supported by straps that came down over the forehead and down the sides of their heads behind their ears. The masks were thus securely fastened over the women's faces, but could be quickly lifted off by the whip-master.

Where the securing straps met on the top of the head was a pretty little red box to which was attached a long red plume like an ostrich feather. Each plume rose up, curling back over the head. The rowers plumes were nodding in perfect time as their heads swayed forwards and back as they rowed to the beat of the boy's drum.

I saw that each rower seemed to be terrified of their huge black whip-master whom they watched out of the

169

corner of their eyes as he slowly walked up and down, whilst they tried to keep their eyes fixed, evidently by order, on the back of the rower ahead. Occasionally, each would daringly sneak a quick glance up at the Bey and his guests, sitting comfortably on the raised poop, their eyes flashing coquettishly up in a glance of dumb appeal. With their faces veiled by their masks, it was only with their eyes and their naked bodies that they could attract attention.

All in unison the women would reach right forward before dipping their oars for the next stroke, in time with the drum. Then straining hard, they would sway right back, their heads up, their breasts bouncing prettily, and their beautifully painted and shaven intimacies, outlined like their eyes and nipples in black kohl, being raised and displayed to the men looking down on them from the poop.

I could see that it was an erotic sight, for as they raised their body lips slightly from the bench, their beauty lips would gently open.

I saw that each woman's intimacies had been made up, or painted, in a slightly different way. It was as if, deprived by their masks of beautifying their faces other than their eyes, each naked woman had instead concentrated on decorating her other mouth and its smooth hairless surroundings in order to attract the attention of her Master. Each would, greatly daring, flash her eyes up at him and not only give her breasts an extra shake but also raise up her intimacies in a submissive gesture of offering herself to him.

I gave a gasp as I thought I recognised, despite their veils, two of the women I saw chained to the oars. Chained just in front of the raised poop appeared to be Inez, the once proud Spanish woman who had constantly reported other women to Bashir Aga for punishment during our journey in the wagon to Hassan Ali's estate.

I had been so jealous of her when the Bey had chosen her, instead of me, as part of his share of the proceeds of the Corso which had captured her. I had assumed that he had chosen her for his harem. Now I remembered his mysterious remark at the time about his whip-master 'being short of a couple of oars'. I realised that he had taken her not for his harem but to be a chained galley slave in his private yacht. Serve her right! Then I noticed, with a shock, that she now seemed to be slightly pregnant. How had this happened, I wondered?

I thought I saw the other girl he had chosen, the petite little French girl Dominique, chained several rows behind Inez, towards the bows amongst several other delicate young girls of her slight build. She too seemed to be with child. I remembered how jealous I had been of her too, chosen as I had thought for the Bey's harem.

Now I understood Hamid Hussein's cryptic remark about soon wishing we were still enjoying a relative life of ease in the 'Silver Cage'. Yes indeed! I realised with another shock that although Isabella and I had been the source of immeasurable delight to the Bey at the banquet the night before, we had not been bought for his harem but merely as his galley slaves.

It was a terrifying prospect. The contrast between the elegantly dressed men sitting in the comfort and shade of the poop deck, and the stark naked white women chained to their oars in the sun down on the rowing benches, was horrifying.

Each woman wore a pretty engraved leather belt that was cut in a series of wide diamond shapes each several inches long and decorated with little metal studs around the edges to keep it stiff. It was evidently fastened tightly together behind each woman's back. In front, two of the diamond shaped pieces of stiff leather, each pressing into the woman's abdomen, met just below her swaying nipples and above her navel. This leather belt with its distinctive metal studs contrasted with each woman's

171

wide shiny brass collar - just like mine. The pretty belts and collars set off the women's bodies and made them seem even more naked - just as had the semi-transparent kaftans of the 'Silver Cage'.

For the next hour the galley appeared to continue to be rowed at varying speeds. I heard orders, I heard the drum beat speed up. I heard the crack of the whip. I heard little cries as the women were evidently kept at full stretch by the Bey to amuse his guests. How I hated him! How I dreaded what was shortly going to happen to me!

The thought of him sitting there in comfort on the cushions in the shade, enjoying seeing the women being flogged into straining at their oars for his amusement, made me furious. I shook the bars of my little cage, but they were solid and strong. There was no escape. I too was going to be forced into becoming one of his pretty branded galley slaves.

The drum beat changed. I heard more orders. It was as if the galley was being manoeuvred by the galley slaves. The drum ceased, and with it the creaking of the oars. I heard a splash as if an anchor had been dropped, then a little jar as if the galley was being moored alongside. I remembered how I'd seen it moored in Hassan Ali's private harbour, with its stern to the jetty, in the typical Mediterranean way of mooring vessels in this tideless and usually calm sea.

Chapter 26

THE SLAVE PENS

Suddenly I felt my cage being lifted up. It seemed as though it was being carried ashore. I heard footsteps echoing as if the men carrying my cage were walking on paving stones inside some building. There was an animal-like smell.

My cage was put down.

The canvas front was lifted up. I could see virtually nothing for two feet in front of the cage was a bare brick wall. At the foot of the wall, cemented into the floor, was a large metal ring with a heavy chain fastened to it.

The footsteps went away, returning a few minutes later, presumably with the cage containing Isabella.

Then the black hands of Bashir Aga unfastened the top of the cage and lifted it up. He reached down and gripped my collar. He quickly locked the heavy chain to the back of it.

"Out!" he ordered brusquely. He pulled me out of the cage by the chain, thrusting the empty cage back into the passageway.

I found that I was kneeling on small paving stones, lightly covered with straw, in what seemed to be a miniature stall similar to those you see in stables. I tried to stand up, but the chain fastened to the back of my collar was only about four feet in length, thus keeping me in a kneeling or squatting position. The stall was about four feet wide and only three feet deep, so that a woman chained within it would have to remain curled up or kneeling.

The stall opened onto a passageway, but was raised two feet above the floor of the passageway so that a woman kneeling in her stall would be easily accessible, without them even bending down, to her overseer or owner standing in the passageway. There was a little raised edge along the side of the stall to prevent the woman from accidentally falling into the passageway. I saw that across the passageway was another raised row of stalls similar to mine, each separated from its neighbour by a high partition, making it impossible for any slave chained in one stall to see or touch a slave woman in the stall next to her.

I had been looking at the wall at the back of my stall at the foot of which was the ring fastened to my collar chain. Along one partition at the side of the stall was two small troughs. One contained water and the other some scraps of rice and bits of food. Fastened to the partition on the other side of the stall was another small water trough evidently intended for washing, for there was a small piece of soap alongside it. Obviously washing was very important for the galley slaves since they would sweat a lot at their oars.

The raised cobbled floor of the stall was slightly sloped towards the centre of the stall where a shallow open channel led to the edge of the stall. The raised edge of the stall had been removed for a few inches where the channel met it, and the lip of the channel projected several inches into the passageway.

The purpose of this arrangement was only too evident and I was blushing with embarrassment as Bashir Aga pointed out that liquids draining from a woman's body between the cobbles and down into the channel would then spill over the lip of the channel and drop down into a larger drain, partly covered with big paving stones, that ran along each side of the passageway, just as in a stable

174

for horses. But I could see that it would be difficult not to wet much of the stall and I wondered about more solid wastes.

Above the washing trough was a small shelf containing a hairbrush and comb and an assortment of little make-up tubs containing rouge, kohl, henna and rice powder. There was also a little mirror.

In the corner was the coloured print of a man wearing Turkish robes, which were flung open disclosing his nakedness and also his impressively erect manhood. He was smiling and looking down at two figures kneeling at his feet in a position of worship. With a shock I saw that they were naked white women and that the man held two chains that were fastened to collars round their necks. The man was unmistakably the Bey. The picture was positioned so that no matter how a woman, chained in her stall, might move about she could not help looking at it. It was certainly erotic and I felt my loins becoming moist as I gazed up at it.

I had to admit that the Bey was a clever swine. The picture was rather like that of a god whom the woman in the stall was to worship in secret, as indeed we all did. We were roused by it, but unable to satisfy ourselves.

I felt my buttocks being tapped firmly by a whip and I looked around in alarm. Bashir Aga was looking down at me, his powerful black arms crossed on his naked chest.

"So you excited by picture of your Master?"

"Oh no, Sir," I gasped.

Quickly he put his hand down between my legs, finding immediately, to my great shame the wet signs of my arousal, the lie to my denial.

"Yes, and he now your Master, little slave! You just one of galley slaves. You start training very soon."

"Oh no!" I moaned in despair.

"Ha! You think he buy you for harem, eh? He like all women first spend little time as galley slaves. Make

175

woman more obedient and make breasts firm. Master like that!"

"A little time?" I seized anxiously on the words like a drowning man grasping a life belt.

"Maybe six months. We see."

"Six months!"

"So, you love Master?"

I did not answer for a moment. I wanted to scream that I hated him. Then, instead I found myself whispering, "Yes, I love him, oh yes!"

"Now you listen carefully. I not repeat orders. Galley slaves sometimes spend all night chained to oars in galley but if back home they sleep here in slave pens. Each slave has own stall, with name."

He pointed to an Arabic sign above my stall, which of course I could not read, for like nearly all white slaves I had been deliberately kept illiterate in Arabic. "Look! This now your name, 'Playful' - Master choose that name specially for you."

"Playful?" I queried.

"Yes, Playful, and your friend now Growler."

"Oh!" I said, shocked into silence. So I was now Playful! That awful Bey knew very well that I was Miss Barbara Kennedy. He was deliberately degrading me by calling me just Playful. How could I have been so stupid as to whisper a moment previously that I loved him! No woman could love such a swine.

"Now listen! Master likes all women keep hair well brushed back and plaited into long pigtail like little girl. Women normally wear masks and headdress plumes in galley. Only sometimes will Master allow veils to be removed so that he can see faces. So very important you make-up body lips and breasts to catch his eye as well as face. You listen carefully or you get whip."

There followed an embarrassingly frank lesson on what the Master would expect to see as he looked down on the naked women. Somehow, even after all that I had experienced, I could not get used to the idea of not merely painting my eyes, but also the more intimate parts of my body, and outlining them with black kohl.

Sometimes the Bey would come to visit his beautified galley slaves, each kneeling prettily and docilely on all fours on the bare cobbles. The Bey would be accompanied not only by Bashir Aga, but also, apparently, by Matrak, the chief black eunuch of his harem. Promotions to the harem were then decided.

My wrist chain was now locked half way along its length to the ring on the front of my slave collar, thus greatly reducing the movement of my hands. Try as I might, I found that I could not reach down below my navel. And a mask was fitted over my face.

I explored my stall. Prevented from standing up by my collar chain, I found that I could crawl around the stall, going to one side to drink and eat and to the other to wash and make-up, and remaining in the centre when using the channel. I could lie down quite comfortably, provided of course that I had not wetted or dirtied any of the straw, but I had to curl up like a dog in his basket.

No matter how I lay or where I crawled, however, I could not prevent my eyes from glancing again and again up at the picture of my Master, his manhood erect with two chained naked white women, kneeling humbly at his feet, just as I was kept kneeling in my stall. I could not help fantasising that I was one of those women at his feet. I remembered the excitement of actually kneeling at his feet at the Banquet. I felt his slave, his humble but joyful slave. He was my Master. I felt again the familiar moist feeling in my loins. Did I, after all, love my Master?

Suddenly Bashir Aga hustled down the passageway where I could see a pair of iron barred gates were fitted, clearly as a security precaution to prevent any woman, who had somehow slipped her collar, from escaping.

I heard him unlock the heavy gates. Then I heard familiar voices approaching, those of the Bey and his two wealthy Arab friends.

So that was why I was masked. Visitors were expected!

Chapter 27

BRANDED!

I heard the chinking of chains, tinkling of bells and the tramp of bare feet. Twenty women, stark naked except for their wide shining brass collars and the leather belts round their waists, were being marched along the passageway by Bashir Aga.

I was to learn that the palace of the Bey, the right hand man of the Pasha of Marsa himself, had been built in the cool of a small promontory sticking out from the town into the bay. His galley was moored stern-on to the palace quay. The slave pens, in which I was now incarcerated, were right next door to where the galley was moored, thus permitting the galley slaves to be quickly marched on and off the vessel itself.

The girls who comprised the Bey's crew were marching in step, their breasts swinging in unison, the bells hanging from their nipple rings tinkling merrily, their eyes fixed straight ahead. As usual, Bashir Aga had a whip in his hand. He cracked it loudly and the girls halted smartly and stood at attention in the passageway between the two lines of stalls.

Then one at a time, Bashir Aga started to call out their names, "Agile! ... Eager! ... Nimble! ... Wilful! ... Placid! ... Dainty! ..." As each woman's slave name was called, she turned and marched smartly to her stall where the drummer boy fastened the heavy chain in each stall to the ring at the back of her collar and her wrist chain to

179

the ring at the front of her collar. They were now chained just like me. He also removed the high red plume from each girl's head mask and then the mask itself, now that there were no strange men to see her face.

As he slipped the mask off one of the pregnant women, I saw that as I had suspected, she was Inez, the once proud Spanish woman who had been so unpopular amongst us for her duplicity. I caught her eye and she flashed me a look of recognition and embarrassment.

When the Negro drummer boy slipped the mask off another girl in the line of pens opposite mine, I saw that she was Dominique, the petite young French girl. Like Inez, her little belly was also well swollen and so too were her breasts. She smiled at me, and I remembered to my shame, how jealous I had been of her when the Bey had picked her out, as I thought, for his harem.

"Eat, Playful, eat!" Quickly I started to gobble up the mixture of rice and bits of vegetables, scraps from the Bey's Palace. Later, after the Bey had dined, the Negro would come down the passageway with a bowl containing scraps of meat left over from the dinner of the Bey and his guests. He would fling little pieces into the stalls of the women whom he felt needed them most. At a word of command they would burrow in their straw to find the scraps of meat, for this was the only meat we received. It was also a powerful incentive to keep one's straw clean and dry.

Included amongst the scraps of meat would be bones which we would chew eagerly and then, like dogs in kennels, hide under the straw to chew again on subsequent nights. How often I would feel very jealous watching a woman across the passageway chewing her bone when I had nothing to chew!

It amused the strict Negro overseer to have twenty young white women all piteously begging him to fling them a scrap of meat or a bone. The cunning Negro would only give each woman just enough to allow her to strain properly at her oar, but not put on any weight.

It was several hours later that the brutal overseer came back and without a word of explanation unfastened Isabella from her stall and led her down the passageway and through the barred gates.

"Silence in the pens!" he ordered as he left.

The women's chattering ceased. No one dared to speak. I heard the drummer boy beginning to beat his drum. After several minutes he stopped and there was a terrible scream. It was Isabella!

A few minutes later she tottered down the passageway dragged along by the Negro. I saw that hanging from each of her nipples was a bell that rang as she staggered. A short silver chain linked her nipples forcing them unnaturally together. Her leather belt had been fastened high around her waist.

I saw that she was desperately trying to reach down with her hands that were still shackled by her wrist chain to her collar. But she could only reach just below her breasts. She was trying to reach the fresh scar of her brand, a green brand, just below her navel, of two crossed scimitars!

Sobbing, she was taken back to her stall, and made to kneel down. Her collar was refastened to the heavy stall chain. She lay curled up, crying and still unable to reach the brand to ease the pain. They did not want her to touch it, of course, in case she spoiled the neat outline. The other women all kept silent. This was clearly part of the ritual, whenever a woman was branded.

Bashir Aga now came slowly towards my stall. The drum started to beat again. I screamed, but the Negro ignored my cries. He unlocked my collar chain and gripped my arm, pulling me to my feet. I struggled but he was so strong I was putty in his hands. He unlocked the first gate and dragged me through it, locking it behind me, before unlocking the second gate.

In a little courtyard was a brazier. Standing by it was something that looked like a hangman's gallows. My heart was in my mouth. Hanging from the top piece, instead of a noose, was a chain. I saw that the coals in the brazier were red hot.

Standing by the brazier was a burly half naked Negro blacksmith with a thick leather apron. Sweat ran down his body from the heat of the brazier.

Squatting in the corner of the courtyard was the Negro boy with his drum, and seated comfortably, away from the heat of the brazier, was the Bey.

I flung myself to his feet.

"Master! Your Highness! Please don't do this to me!" I sobbed these words repeatedly as I humbly licked his feet and his shoes, occasionally looking up at him appealingly.

He made no reply. I saw the blacksmith remove the branding iron from the brazier: it looked red hot. I screamed piteously, but the drum smothered my screams.

Bashir Aga picked me up off my knees and fastened me by my manacles to the chain hanging from the gallows. He pulled the other end of the chain and soon I was hanging with only my toes touching the ground. He reached into the brazier and pulled out a long needle. The Negro boy started to beat a faster tattoo on his drum.

"Keep quite still or you get hurt!" Bashir Aga said. But hanging as I was, I could scarcely move anyway. He squeezed my right nipple. I could feel it becoming erect. I looked down and saw him deftly drive the needle through it, opening up again my former infibulation holes. I gave a scream, but again it was drowned by the drum. He put the needle back into the brazier and threaded a small silver ring through the hole in my nipple. Then he picked up another tool from the brazier and soldered the ends together. Then he picked up a bell just like the one I'd seen the other women wear. He hung it from the ring and squeezed the ends of the supporting ring together so that I would not be able to remove that either. He let it go and stood back to admire his work. It would ring with the slightest movement of my body.

Then Bashir Aga fastened a short silver chain to my nipple rings. It was very tight and pulled my breasts closer together. The drag on my sore nipples hurt painfully. He shook his head.

"Too tight for now. Maybe later."

I saw the Bey nod his head. The Negro slipped off the chain, and replaced it with another, very slightly longer. It was still tight but it let my breasts hang more naturally and did not hurt so much.

"That better!" he said. He beckoned to the blacksmith. Horrified I saw him pick up a red hot iron and put it up to my breasts. I did not dare move. Gently he held the iron up to the clip on each end of the chain that fastened it to my nipple rings and soldered over the join. The chain was now fixed, pulling my breasts gently together. It was a strange and rather exciting feeling, knowing that I could not remove the chain any more than I could remove the bells.

Then, to my horror, I saw the blacksmith go to the brazier and remove the brand. I realised that it would have cooled in being used on poor Isabella and had now heated up again satisfactorily. The Bey nodded to Bashir Aga who went behind me, pushing my naked belly towards the blacksmith.

"I told you in Malta, Miss Kennedy, that you might end up as a slave in Barbary. And now here you are, a slave, my slave, my property, my galley slave ..." He watched as the blacksmith drove the brand against my belly. I remembered that the drum had stopped. I remember hearing myself scream and scream through the smoke, as he held the brand against my belly for several seconds which felt like hours.

Shocked and in terrible pain, I scarcely noticed as Bashir Aga fastened the uniform leather belt high around my waist above the brand. The belt made me keep in my tummy, making my nakedness a yet prettier sight from the poop deck, or when kneeling in my stall. As it was, my brand dominated my thoughts, the pain from my brand.

Bashir Aga, using a brush, scattered green paint powder into the open wound of the brand, to make it show up more noticeably once it had healed. I had wondered why the other womens' brands and marks had been such a bright green in colour, such a distinctive colour on a white skin: now I knew.

Then he rubbed a strange ointment into the brand. I thought it was a healing ointment to ease the pain but, on the contrary, it made it burn all the more - it must delay the healing process and thus make the scar all the more noticeable.

I was sobbing with pain as my arms were let down from the gallows. My wrist manacles were fastened to the ring in the front of my collar. Desperately I tried to reach down to my brand. But, of course I could not reach it. Sobbing like Isabella had done, I was taken back to my stall and my collar fastened to the chain again.

For the next three days Isabella and I were kept in our stalls while our brands slowly healed, the process carefully delayed by Bashir Aga's horrible ointment. On the third day, one of the galley slaves was promoted to the Bey's harem and another given away to one of his retainers as a present. Apparently the fact that she bore the Bey's brand made her even more valuable, just as the mark of a well known collector increases the value of a picture. Allowing for the spare girls that Bashir Aga always liked to keep in his team of galley slaves, there was now room for Isabella and me.

During those three days I had had plenty of time to reflect on my new position as one of he Bey's branded galley slaves. As I looked down on the slowly healing brand, I knew that I hated him more than I had ever hated anyone. I belonged utterly and irrevocably to him, and for the rest of my life I would carry his brand mark.

I was one of his women!

Yet somehow it seemed only right and proper that such a dominant and wealthy man should have so many women. Somehow I felt proud to be one of them.

Then, on the third day, Isabella and I were marched out with the other galley slaves to his galley and chained to an oar.

Chapter 28

LIFE AS A GALLEY SLAVE

I had now been a galley slave in the Bey's private galley for a couple of months. It was difficult to know just how long, since we were not allowed any writing materials and had no way of noting the passing of time. Certainly the winter rains seemed to have passed and the sun was hotter, making me sweat profusely at my oar. My body was also becoming deeply tanned.

At first I could not believe that any delicate young European woman could survive the harshness with which the Bey's female galley slaves were treated. But I had been surprised how quickly my muscles had got used to the way, naked and exposed to both the rain and sun, we were made to toil at our oars by the threat of the whip of Bashir Aga.

I looked up at the poop. There was hatred in my eyes. At least I think there was hatred, but it might equally well have been respect, or even love - the sort of dumb appealing love that you see in a dog looking up at a strict but beloved master. For there, standing on the poop deck and gripping the rail as he looked down, was the Bey himself.

I well remembered having to sit silently chained to my oar all one long rainy night, moored off the luxurious villa of a rich Turkish widow with whom he was spending the night. It seemed that he would think nothing of keeping twenty beautiful young galley slaves up all night, and of deserting a similar number of women in his harem, simply for the excitement of chasing a new and attractive free woman.

I well remembered my tense embarrassment and jealousy one evening when he brought her for a romantic cruise.

In her magnificent Turkish dress, covered in priceless jewels, she accompanied the Bey along the catwalk of the galley to inspect us naked galley slaves. One by one, we had to raise our belly, bearing the Bey's branded crest, up towards her for her inspection. Then we had to kneel up on our benches to lick her exquisite little Turkish slippers, whilst she gave the Bey a candid criticism of each of us in turn. Of me, she had said, 'This little slut is clearly in love with you. She is like a moonstruck servant girl, which she probably was before she was a slave'

I saw the Bey smile. He told her that I was an Irish governess. She smiled cruelly. I hated her! I hated her for her rich clothes and jewels; I hated her for her freedom; I hated her for the way my Master seemed to respect her. I hated her for the contemptuous way in which she had spoken of me, but I just had to sit on my bench, my arms stretched out straight in front of me, my hands gripping my oar, my eyes fixed straight ahead of me, trying not to sob.

I had to learn the complicated rowing drills. For instance, I had to learn the six short quick strokes used to get the galley moving initially, and then the next ten strokes during which we had to slowly extend the length of each stroke until each girl was reaching right forward, and then, in time with the beat of the drum, pulling her oar right back as far as she could go without falling off her bench.

I had to learn to take my time from the drum, or from the girls at the two stroke oars, seated at the foot of the short ladder that led up to the poop deck.

I also had to learn to respond instantly to changes in speed. One moment we might be rowing steadily at a medium or slow speed, and then at a sign from the Arab coxswain, or from the Bey himself, the drummer boy would beat a double tattoo on his drum, and start speeding up the rate of strokes while Bashir Aga would apply his whip to our backs.

A spell of rowing at full speed was utterly exhausting, and only the whip could make you maintain it for any length of time. You would be longing for the double tattoo on the drum which would signal relaxing again to a slower speed.

The constant changes in speed were a deliberate way of getting us fit. I remembered how with horses back in Ireland the best way of getting them fit was by constantly changing speed from a walk to a short gallop, and then back to a trot, followed by another short gallop or slowing down to a walk. There was no steady routine, so the horse never knew what speed would be coming next. But his muscles would be getting stronger and stronger.

We had to learn the complicated manoeuvres required for quickly mooring the vessel stern on to the quay at the foot of the Bey's Palace, or to other jetties. The coxswain would order the oars on one side to hold water, or back water whilst the oars on the other side would be pulling hard, so that the galley would spin round in a small area. We had to learn how to back water and then how to hold water with our oars to stop the galley. It was all quite difficult and woe betide any girl who got it wrong - Bashir Aga's whip would be across her breasts in a flash.

It was indeed extraordinary how that cunning Negro could tell when a girl was secretly trying to take things easy by going through the motions of pulling her oar without actually pulling her full weight. He could tell

188

from the way the muscles on a girl's back were moving whether or not she was really straining her utmost. And if she wasn't, then he would be on to her like a hawk, his whip flailing her back.

It was horrible, feeling that that your body was being controlled by the drum and the whip.

Each day would start in the pens at dawn.

We would hear the noise of Bashir Aga's key in the two metal grilles that closed off the pens. Then he would come striding proudly down the passageway. This jet black, ugly looking, powerfully built eunuch was indeed proud to be Whipmaster of the personal galley of His Excellency Hussein Bey, the local Commander of the Janissaries of His Imperial Majesty, the Sultan of Turkey.

His pride stemmed not only from his position, but also from his success in keeping the young women in his charge at a constant peak of physical fitness. There would be complete silence as he slowly walked down the central passageway, his short whip in his hand, his cunning little eyes glancing searchingly at the women displaying themselves either side of the passageway.

His whip would be deliberately much in evidence. It was, indeed, the constant sight of the whip, and the sound of its frequent and terrifying cracking, that induced the fear that was the keystone of his training methods.

Just as a successful trainer of race horses knows everything about the physical condition of his horses, so Bashir Aga knew all about the physical state of the female galley slaves in his charge.

Soon, each woman, now kneeling sideways on to the passageway in her stall, was hungrily eying the porridge in her feeding trough, and eagerly awaiting the order to start eating.

The porridge itself was made from a mixture of boiled oats and barley with a sprinkling of little pieces of fresh fruit. It was well salted to replace the salt that we would lose as we perspired at our oars. It had the advantage of being cheap and yet nutritious.

Bashir Aga would crack his whip and two dozen pretty young faces would be lowered into their troughs, eagerly swallowing and guzzling up the horrid mash just like animals. Each woman knew that woe betide any galley slave who had not eaten up her allotted ration and licked her trough clean by the time he cracked his whip again. Then he would come down the line of stalls, checking that each trough was spotlessly clean. He would give a grunt of satisfaction. We were very well trained!

Then came the noise of a large wheel barrow being trundled down the corridor by the Bey's head gardener. He had come to collect the slaves' daily offerings, which played an important role in the growth of the many beautiful flowers that abounded in the Palace gardens and patios.

As the now full wheel barrow was trundled away by the satisfied head gardener, the drummer boy would now go down the line of galley slaves unlocking each woman's wrist manacles from the ring on the front of her collar. As he did so, each girl would stretch out her hands with a feeling of pure delight. But Bashir Aga would be watching to make certain that the girls only used this moment of freedom to titivate their faces and, above all, their eyes and their beauty lips. Each would be desperately anxious to paint them so as to catch the Bey's eye. Marsa was a world in which often the difference for a woman between success and abject failure depended on the curl of her eyelashes.

Before actually starting to paint ourselves we had to wash with water from the other special bowl in our stalls. Then we had to wash, brush and comb our hair.

When Bashir Aga was satisfied with the appearance of the women under his command, our neck chains would be removed and we would fall in in two lines in the passageway. At a word of command we would march off and moments later the drummer boy would be locking each of our wrist manacles to the metal clasp in the loom of our oar, ready for another day's work.

Chapter 29

USED FOR THE BEY'S PLEASURE

A day came when Bashir Aga suddenly took me from my oar. Then, watched jealously by all the other women, he took me along the catwalk and up onto the poop deck to put my head under the Bey's robe. The other women were kept rowing at full stretch for his further pleasure.

I well remember the feeling of excitement and fear as I crawled up the companionway to the poop, and my feeling of intense disappointment, a few minutes later, when, having brought him to the very point of climaxing, he kicked me aside and ordered Bashir Aga to replace me with another girl, and then another and another. Each had to bring him almost to the height of arousal as we sped back to his Palace, but he was clearly keeping himself for his harem, and merely using us as a little appetizer.

It was a scene that would be repeated frequently - much to my frustration and that of the other women.

But I also remember how thrilled I was when he ordered Bashir Aga to take me down to his luxurious small cabin under the poop to share his bed for the night as the galley was rowed by the other women along the coast to the village he was due to inspect the following day. I well remember my shame and disappointment when Bashir Aga chained me by the neck to the foot of the bed, so that when my Master came into the bed and lay back to be pleased, my head was only level with his waist and was completely hidden beneath the bedclothes.

Our Negro overseer had warned me, silently pointing to his whip, always to address the Bey as 'Your Excellency, my Master'. However, I had no opportunity to speak to him. I was simply a hidden, silent and anonymous giver of pleasure. I did not dare to say a word, and remained completely frustrated. Indeed there was no sign that he knew, or cared, who was pleasing him under the bedclothes until, just as he reached his climax he flung them back, gripped my head tightly by my hair and bringing his dog whip down hard and across my naked back, murmured ecstatically, "That's very good, little Barbara Kennedy. You're a good little bitch."

During my time in the 'Silver Cage' I had frequently been allowed a little pleasure, and become accustomed to it. Now giving pleasure, whilst remaining totally frustrated oneself, was a new experience, though one that we had been taught in Hassan Ali's school to expect from a private Master.

I realised that my Master was deliberately showing off his complete control of my body to heighten my feeling of being his abject slave. He was deliberately making me keep all my energy for pulling my oar in his accursed galley! I found my enforced purity gave the act of swallowing his seed an almost religious aspect, and made me adore him, whilst still hating him for his cruelty.

I must have pleased the Bey quite a lot, for thereafter he often sent for me when he was on board for his afternoon siesta, but always with Madame de Savoury, his new French favourite, or with Inez whom I hated of old.

They were not chained down, like me, under the bedclothes. It made me even more jealous of them. Why shouldn't I be allowed to lie in his arms like them? Why must I always be chained down to the foot of the bed like a dog? I had to compete against Madame de Savoury or Inez to give him pleasure, and yet they were allowed a head start. The could kiss him, tickle his chin with their tongues and whisper sweet nothings to him, whilst my chain only just enabled me to reach up to his thighs. It wasn't fair! And worst of all was when I could see his hand reaching down to excite them - though he kept me completely frustrated.

It was when I was chained down under the bedclothes one day that I saw that Madame de Savoury bore on her belly, not the brand mark of the Bey, but that of the Pasha.

Of course, it was rare for the Bey to use any of us galley slaves for his real enjoyment. Normally he slept, both at night and during the hot afternoons, in his harem with his concubines. Meanwhile at night we galley slaves slept on a thin layer of straw in our pens, and during his siesta we sat exposed to the hot sun and chained to our oars. In both cases we were unable to touch ourselves and thinking of him and his manhood, and of the way in which he might that very moment be making love to his other women, was terribly frustrating.

But my daydreams of lying in his arms were often harshly interrupted. The Negro's whip would suddenly come down across my back, the knotted tip coming up under my outstretched arms as I reached forward for the next stroke and catching me painfully across the breasts. Bashir Aga was certainly an expert in driving women with his whip without hurting them sufficiently to make them fail to keep in stroke, or leave a permanent mark on their skins.

"Go on, little Playful, go on! Pull harder! Master bought you to pull his galley, not to play with your oar!"

Then he would move on silently down the catwalk behind me. I did not know if he was still watching me or not. I would pull my oar back harder, straining every muscle, for fear that his eye might be on me again. I would sway right back on my bench, keeping my back straight and my head up, just as he had taught me. I would pull the loom of the oar back to my breasts, making my nipple bells ring prettily in time of those of the other women, and I would raise my branded belly and my painted beauty lips up towards my Master, sitting relaxed on the poop deck. Then, in perfect time with the other women, I would sway forward, once again the notes from my nipple rings mixing musically with those of the others.

"Better!" I might unexpectedly hear the black overseer's voice behind me. "Not dare slack again!"

As well as looking down on us from the poop as we rowed, and occasionally summoning one or more of us to please him on the poop deck itself, or in his cabin immediately below it, the Bey would also enjoy an occasional walk along the catwalk. Grinning as he showed off his charges, the brutal Bashir Aga would accompany him, his whip at the ready, like an animal trainer might show off his cowering animals to a circus owner. The Bey would slowly make his way along the catwalk, standing over each woman in turn as she strained at her oar.

I remember the first time he came to me, I was trying hard to keep my eyes firmly fixed on the back of the woman immediately in front of me. I knew I would have to keep silent as he discussed me with his overseer ...

"Yes, Your Excellency, this one now one month at oars. She scared of whip, but still lazy if I not watch her!"

It was not true, I longed to cry out in protest! I had been pulling my heart out for my Master. How unfair the black eunuch was! Surely my Master must have noticed how I had been pulling my oar desperately hard just to please him.

"Lazy? Then use the whip more on her," came the angry voice of the Bey.

195

Then he passed on to the next woman, leaving me terrified. Indeed, the next few days were ghastly. No matter how hard I tried, the eunuch's whip was always driving me on to greater efforts.

Two days later, the Bey stood over me again, as petrified, I strained at my oar.

I felt him trace the mark of the eunuch's whip across my shoulders with his quirt, the local Arab riding whip which he always carried.

"I'm glad to see you've been standing no more nonsense from this one," he remarked casually to Bashir Aga. His quirt ran down the front of my shoulders. It touched my breasts. They were still tender from the recent attentions of the dreaded eunuch's whip. "I can see that her breasts are getting tauter and firmer. Well done Bashir Aga!"

Well done, I thought bitterly! What has the eunuch got to do with it?

Sometimes, when the Bey was not in a hurry to be taken back across the bay to his Palace, he would order us to stop rowing before he came down to inspect us. We had to hold our oars stiffly in front of us, our arms reaching forward, our bodies erect.

How I remember the first time he felt me. He had stopped by me, and after looking my body up and down, had felt my breasts. I was overcome with shame and excitement. I could feel myself blushing as I kept my eyes fixed on the back of the girl in front of me. But I also felt a moist heat in my loins.

"They still aren't very big, Bashir Aga," I heard him remark. "Perhaps we should consider taking some special steps to improve matters!"

"Please no, Your Excellency!" I burst out.

Then, overcome with the realisation of what I had done in speaking to my Master without permission, I quickly turned my head back to look straight in front of me and gasped, "Oh, I'm sorry Sir, I'm sorry! I did not mean ..."

To speak to the Master without permission was classed as Impertinence, and the punishment could be very severe. What a fool I had been! I sat there trembling with fear at what might happen to me. There was complete silence, broken only by the tinkling of my heavy nipple bells as my breasts rose and fell in my agitation. After what seemed to be hours, I heard the Bey's voice.

"I don't think she meant to be impertinent, Bashir Aga, but I really can't have them interrupting me. I think three strokes will suffice this time."

I felt Bashir Aga grasp my hair, holding me quite still. Then he brought his whip down under my outstretched arms, right across both my breasts. I gave a gasp of pain. I longed to scream, to cry out for mercy, to beg for no more, but I knew that I had to keep quite quiet and wait submissively for the second and the third excruciating strokes. Suddenly they came, harder than the first. I only just prevented myself from screaming with the pain.

How could I be more submissive, more adoring, more obedient! Sir, I longed to scream out, I'll make you a wonderful concubine. I'll live only to please you, my beloved Master.

Now his hand was arousing me steadily. I could hardly keep still. My beauty bud was aching to rub itself against his hand. If my hands had not been chained to my oar, I could not have stopped myself from curling up and gripping his wrist to make him stroke me faster and faster. But the Bey, whilst keeping his hand moving only very slowly was talking to the brutal Negro about other things, and I was ignored, left more frustrated than ever.

Chapter 30

SENT TO THE BEY'S HAREM

The day of what we had been told was to be an important race was evidently getting closer. However, we were deliberately kept ignorant about just when it was to be.

Bashir Aga had got us all fighting fit, and welded into a well disciplined and highly efficient team. Whenever we were not needed to take the Bey on some urgent business around the harbour, we would be kept pulling steadily at our oars for increasingly long periods.

Several times we were made to practice rowing all night. It was an exhausting experience. We soon learned to take advantage of short stops to sleep sitting at our benches, and then refreshed to row again for several hours in the darkness.

Often the Bey himself would take time off from his busy official activities to put us through our paces - pointing out to Bashir Aga any woman who seemed to need more attention from his whip.

It was now summer and thirst was a terrible problem. We were not allowed to drink very much, even before going on board, lest we hold up the galley by needing to squat over the brass bowl. Often, when I thought I was going to die from thirst, the drummer boy would thrust a slice of lemon or a handful of dates between my eager lips.

We would return to our stalls exhausted, and longing to be allowed to curl up and sleep. It had been sheer hell when we were then called out during the night to take the Bey on some unexpected business, or to deliver an urgent message by sea.

One day we saw that a large crowd was lining the shore. It was the race day! The umpire, an Arab doctor, had previously checked that the number of slaves pregnant met the race conditions. He had weighed each of us and noted the slave numbers tattooed on our forearms. He now came on board to check that no changes had been made.

I could see that a dozen other galleys, all with women galley slaves, and flying numerous brightly coloured flags, were lining up for the start. Over the top of the bulwarks I saw the wretched women in the galleys of the Arab chiefs against whom we were to race. I saw the team of one had a white bleached streak in their hair which gave them all a strangely similar look. I saw another galley manned entirely by much younger women, and was horrified to think that they too had been made to meet the race requirements of half of the slaves being with child. I saw another galley in which all the women had large ear rings that hung down to their shoulders.

I will not dwell upon the terrible race; the the sheer agony of having to row for hours and hours on end, driven on by fear of the whip; having to keep going throughout the night whilst the Master and the coxswain, and Bashir Aga or the drummer boy, took it in turns to sleep; or the clever way in which Bashir Aga and our Master conserved our rapidly flagging energies right to the end, making us give a final burst at full speed that left us absolutely exhausted, but which put us just ahead of our rivals.

Our Master was delighted with his win. We saw the pile of gold coins being handed over. We had made our Master richer! As a reward we were each allowed a piece of Turkish Delight in our feed and left to sleep for a whole day!

Our Master gave a banquet in his Palace on the water's edge to celebrate his victory, the highlight of which was the sight of us rowing the galley slowly past and then returning at full speed - with the galley beautifully lit up with flaming torches.

The weekly inspection on the Friday following the race would, we all knew, be of great importance. The Bey was now free to promote some galley slaves to his harem, to purchase replacements, to sell off those women who he no longer wanted, and to send unfit concubines from his harem back to the galley as a punishment.

I was petrified as I knelt on all fours in my stall as the Bey passed slowly down the passage. I did not dare even flicker my eyes towards him, but kept them rigidly fixed on the wall in front of me, hoping that I was giving an impression of obedience and humility - the two attributes that I had learned the Bey most appreciated in a woman.

Out of the corner of my eye, I saw his Turkish slippers stop by my stall, and held my breath. There was a pause which seemed to go on for ever. I was pulling in my belly, and thrusting out my buttocks in a desperate attempt to make myself look as attractive to him as possible. I could feel the heat in my loins spreading as his eyes wandered over my naked body, inspecting me.

I raised my eyes like a little dog to my Master's stern face. I saw him turn to Bashir Aga and nod. Then he moved on down the passageway, leaving me tense and nervous.

Half an hour later, Bashir Aga came and unfastened my collar chain. Stark naked, I was led down the passageway and into the room where I had been branded. A huge Negro stood there, a cruel smile on his lips. He was Matrak, the Bey's chief black eunuch, in charge of his harem, and my heart started to beat faster.

I saw Bashir Aga show Matrak a little ██████
embarrassed, I realised, as he read out parts ██████
was a record of my most intimate bodily detai███
habits, wastes and monthly cycles. Then, as th███
to discuss this, I had to part my legs and bend my███
for Matrak to inspect me.

My wrist chain was then removed, the retaining riv███
being beaten out with a special hammer. I was amaze███
Surely all slave women in Marsa have to wear a wrist
chain, I thought. Matrak must have guessed my
thoughts.

"Master not make concubines in harem wear wrist
chains!" he said. "Plenty bars on windows and door
guarded, so no escape. But still wear collar with his
name and you still branded with his mark!

But now I really was going to the harem of my beloved
Master! I was so thrilled and excited that I felt like kissing
the black feet of Matrak, but before I could do any such
thing, he fastened a long silky kaftan over me. It was the
first garment that I had worn for months. I stroked it
lovingly with my now free hands, and looked up eagerly
at the huge Negro. He took the little book from Bashir
Aga, and beckoned me to follow him.

And so I entered the harem of my countryman Rory
Fitzgerald, the Bey, the Turkish vice-governor of Marsa,
my Master and my love.

Chapter 31

THE MASTER RETURNS

Suddenly there was the clatter of horse hoofs.

It came from the only window in the harem that looked out onto the outside world - or rather onto the entrance to the Bey's Palace. Heavy wooden lattice work made it impossible, for a man looking up from the Palace courtyard towards the horizontal slit of a window to see anything behind it, and in particular, made it impossible to see the faces of any of us concubines. The very narrowness of the slit, and the bars on the inside, made it impossible for anyone to get into the harem through it, or for any one of the concubines in the harem to try and escape through it.

We were not even allowed to look through the slit without the express permission of Matrak. The approach to the slit was corded off to prevent any of us from obtaining an unauthorized look at another man. The only man we were allowed to see was the Bey and when, as at present, he was away, we were not allowed to catch even a glimpse of another man. In this way, Matrak would be sure that, even against our will, our minds were concentrated on thinking about our Master, with his dramatic good looks and commanding presence.

There were more hoof beats. Two dozen beautiful young women looked up, glancing at each other inquisitively. The Bey had been away for two weeks, two long weeks. Was he now returning? I heard several of the women catch their breath, their breasts suddenly rising and falling anxiously under their pretty coloured boleros.

Slowly we watched Matrak come down from the podium from which he could look down on all the concubines in his charge. He was a huge and hideous figure, wearing full long robes and a white conical hat. In his hand he carried his wand of office: a thin swishy bamboo cane with a flattened silver tip. Although we concubines were only occasionally thrashed, the constant sight of the bamboo cane was a most effective way of keeping discipline in the harem and of ensuring that even his most gently murmured orders were obeyed with alacrity by all of us!

Matrak walked slowly to the window. He unfastened the cord that barred our approach to it and looked out. There was complete silence in the harem as all the women watched him anxiously. Slowly he turned round towards us all.

"Come little girls," he murmured softly. "Come and look at your Master returning to his Palace."

We all rushed forwards, our hearts beating fast. We knelt down, for the slit was only a few inches off the floor. Desperately we each fought to get a place. I squeezed through two other girls and gripped the heavy cast iron bars in front of the slit. On either side of me the other concubines were holding their breath with excitement, as the Bey, our Master, slowly rode into the Palace courtyard, a white pageboy running at each stirrup and another holding a large sun umbrella over him.

He rode erect on his horse, a figure of manliness and virility. There was a deep sigh of desire from the watching women.

One pageboy knelt down in the dust of the courtyard, making a back onto which the Master dismounted. He stood there, a gorgeous figure in his splendid Janissary uniform and large turban, with the jewelled handle of a dagger protruding from the sash round his waist.

We could see he was giving orders in his usual commanding way. There was no other man in the courtyard, only the Bey and his white eunuch pageboys, which was why Matrak had allowed us to watch. The women were all pressing against the bars to get a better view of their Master, the only man they would ever be allowed to speak to and touch. I could not help myself being carried away by the feeling of excitement that was sweeping all the concubines. There was a strong smell of female arousal: my loins were wet with excitement.

We watched as the Bey walked slowly up the steps of the Palace, his head raised high, an arrogant look on his handsome face, his mouth set in a stern expression, over his small pointed beard, his piercing eyes rose momentarily towards the trellis-covered slit as if he knew that we, his concubines, were watching him, each one panting with desire and hope.

He snapped his fingers. A fawning white pageboy fell to his knees and offered him a silver tray containing a glass of refreshing sherbet. The gestures of complete dominance and complete subservience, made each of the women remember a more personal scene, when, in response to a similar snap of his fingers, she had crawled to his feet or under his robe.

"You lucky girls, to have such a handsome Master," cried Matrak, now motioning us back from the window. "Now you get yourselves ready for parade!"

With little excited squeals the women all rushed towards the alcove of Jasmine, the harem hairdresser, each desperately anxious to out do her rivals and make herself more attractive than them so as to catch the eye of their Master.

Would I be chosen?

EPILOGUE BY HUSSEIN BEY

Yes, she was chosen - though in the company of Henrietta and her pretty younger sister, Emma. Indeed, all three of them are now being trained by Matrak to work as one delightful British team, dedicated to giving me even greater pleasure.

I decided it would indeed be amusing to make Barbara write a description of all that had happened to her since we first met in Malta.

I had her shut away by Matrak until she had finished it.

The manuscript gives an amusing little account of the way in which even the most independently minded young European woman can be tamed by a touch of slavery - and even enjoy it.

It paints me as a pretty good swine in my attitude to women. Perhaps I am. But such is the way of the Orient.

One thing I do know - what man would want to return to European ways after living the life that I have become accustomed to - the life that Barbara has described for me?

*** *** *** ***

For specimen chapters and publication details of forthcoming Silver Moon titles please leave name and address on our 24 hour phone line.

(No charge other than phone call)

0891 - 310976

(Calls charged at 36p per min Off Peak: 48p per min at all other times)

or write to:

Silver Moon Readers Services, P.O. Box CR25, Leeds LS7 - 3TN

(New Authors Welcomed)